Her Name Was Lola

NOVELS

The Lion of Boaz-Jachin and Jachin-Boaz
Kleinzeit
Turtle Diary
Riddley Walker
Pilgermann
The Medusa Frequency
Fremder
Mr Rinyo-Clacton's Offer
Angelica's Grotto
Amaryllis Night and Day
The Bat Tattoo

POETRY

The Pedalling Man
The Last of the Wallendas and Other Poems

COLLECTIONS

The Moment Under the Moment

FOR CHILDREN

The Mouse and His Child
The Frances Books
The Trokeville Way

Her Name Was Lola

RUSSELL HOBAN

BLOOMSBURY

First published in Great Britain 2003

Bloomsbury Publishing Plc, 38 Soho Square, London W1D 3HB

A CIP catalogue record for this book is available from the British Library

All papers used by Bloomsbury Publishing are natural, recyclable products
made from wood grown in sustainable, well-managed forests. The
manufacturing processes conform to the environmental regulations of the
country of origin.

ISBN 0 7475 7024 8

10 9 8 7 6 5 4 3 2 1

Typeset by Palimpsest Book Production Limited,
Polmont, Stirlingshire

Printed in Great Britain by Clays Ltd, St Ives plc

ACKNOWLEDGEMENTS

The Garibaldi Restaurant and the Diamond Heart Centre exist only in my imagination. For help with the real world I owe thanks to:

John Guy of the Far Eastern Department of the Victoria and Albert Museum for Apasmara sources.

Gundula, my wife, for advice on Lola's wardrobe and various London sites.

Catherine Frost of the Dorset County Museum and her family for Maiden Castle photographs and notes; John Meyer of Guy Salmon Jaguar for E-type background; Robert Massey of the Greenwich Observatory for astronomical data; the Dorset police for procedural information; my son, Dr Ben Hoban, for medical facts.

Shambhu and Punita Gupta of Indian Music Promotions for descriptions and demonstrations of traditional instruction in Indian classical music and the sarod; Iseabail Macleod of Scottish Language Dictionaries for dialect assistance; Charles Simpson of the Registration Office of Buckie for information on wedding permissions.

Carole Lee for details of Grace Kowalski's workroom.

Dominic Power for readings of successive drafts and useful comments.

To Dominic
(a.k.a. Seamus Flannery)

'The sun rises in the morning,
you run your ship aground,
you get court-martialled.'

Commander Richard Farrington
Captain, HMS *Nottingam*
8 July 2002

CONTENTS

I

NOT A DOG, NOT A CAT

November 2001. No letters on the mat this morning. Thirty or forty flyers for Thai, Chinese, Indian takeaway, Pizza, Painting & Decorating, various car services but no letters. Was there something yesterday? Max can't remember.

He goes down to the kitchen for breakfast, then up to his desk. He turns on the modem and computer, checks his e-mail. One offer to make him a millionaire, one to make his penis three to four inches longer overnight. He trashes both, then looks at what he did yesterday. Max writes novels that don't sell, children's picture books that do. His last novel, *Any That You Cannot Put Downe*, was published eight years ago. He's been working every day but he hasn't got anything that looks like Page One of a new novel. On the children's book front he's also without a Page One. He's had considerable success with a series about a hedgehog called Charlotte Prickles but at the moment Charlotte isn't telling him anything.

'Give it a rest,' says his mind. 'We have a lunch date.' It's almost time to leave so Max puts his Underground book in his rucksack: *A Beleagured City and Other Tales of the Seen and the Unseen* by Margaret Oliphant. Also two videos lent by his friend Seamus Flannery, *Living in Oblivion* and *Being John Malkovich*, and off he goes. To Earls Court on the District Line, then the Piccadilly to Russell Square. Max has got a seat and is absorbed in *A Beleagured City*. In it a dark cloud separates the city of Semur from the daylight around it and the inhabitants are driven out by the invisible presences of the dead. 'Absent friends,' says Max's mind.

'Why did you say that?' says Max.

'I don't know,' says his mind. 'Don't let me distract you from your book.'

Max comes out of Russell Square station and heads for Southampton Row and Il Fornello where he's going to meet Seamus for lunch. Just then the world becomes not there and he has to stop in his tracks while he sees nothing but moving shapes of black. 'Shit,' he says.

'Try to be calm,' says his mind. 'Just stand there until the world comes back.'

Max stands there for what seems a long time. The shapes of black keep moving and changing. The way they do it scares him. He'd like to think it's his mind playing up but this feels as if it's coming from somewhere else. The black shapes are as sharp as double-edged razor blades and Max fears that if he makes a wrong move blood will come out of his eyes and ears and nose and mouth. What would be a wrong move? A wrong thought? He pays close attention to the shapes of black. The distances between them are not always the same. A woman he can't see touches his arm and says, 'Are you all right?'

'I'm OK, thanks,' he says. 'I was just trying to remember if I turned off the cooker.'

'And did you?'

'Not sure but I'll find out when I get home.'

'Good luck,' says the woman, and she's gone.

Is one of the black shapes moving away from the others? Is it something recognisable? Suddenly the world comes back. With a stench of desolation. It smells like a backed-up toilet in an empty house with broken windows. Out of the corner of his eye Max sees something following him. Is it a dog? A cat? It's a little man, black as ebony, long body, very short arms and legs, large head, big ugly baby-face. He's inching along on his belly and writhing like a dog that's been run over. Max looks around. Lots of foot traffic but nobody is stepping on the dwarf. Nobody is taking any notice at all. The smell is almost making Max throw up but he wants to do the decent thing. He says to the dwarf, 'Are you all right?'

'Closer,' says the dwarf. His voice is like dead leaves skittering on the floor of that empty house with the backed-up toilet.

'Not sure this is a good idea,' says Max's mind.

Max comes closer. Like a jumping spider the dwarf springs off the pavement and there he is in Max's arms. 'Hold me,' he says, sobbing a little. This is a very heavy dwarf. Max tries to put him down but his arms and hands have lost the ability to let go.

Again Max looks around. Again nobody's taking any notice. 'OK,' he says to the dwarf. 'Nobody else can see you. Nobody else can hear you. Probably they can't smell you either. You're a hallucination.'

'So?' says the dwarf. He sniffles, belches, farts, then like a baby he goes to sleep in Max's arms. What about the razor blades? Still there? Max isn't sure.

'Now what?' he says to his mind.

'I don't know,' says his mind. 'We'll just have to play it by ear.'

'And nose,' says Max.

Max can't put the dwarf down but he manages to sling him over his shoulder like a sack of potatoes. He moves on, rounds the corner into Southampton Row. Now it's a beautiful blue-sky day. The Russell Hotel looking absolutely real. Fresh wind blowing brown leaves from Russell Square. Hard sunlight glinting off the traffic. Tourists thick on the ground. Young ones with backpacks as big as steamer trunks, mineral water, London maps. Old ones with trolley bags. Ordinarily Max wishes they'd go away. Today he'd like to see more of them. The London Pride sightseeing bus is waiting for punters in its usual place. The luggage shop a little farther along is offering backpacks and trolley bags at SALE prices. The shop that sells electronic marvels of all kinds is flaunting its hand-held DVD players and other erotica. So things are fairly normal but although the sunlight is hard and bright there doesn't seem to be enough light in the day for Max.

At Il Fornello he gets a hearty greeting from the staff. '*Dottore* Max!' says Bruno at the till. 'How are you?' Max isn't a doctor but at Il Fornello any regular patron over forty is *Dottore* and those over sixty are *Professore*. '*Dottore!*' says Juliano, coming to shake his hand. 'Have you hurt your back?'

'Heavy lifting,' says Max. He wonders if he'll be able to put the dwarf down to take his jacket off. Bad move? Paco comes to help him. The dwarf wakes up, drops to the floor, waits until the jacket is hung up, then he does his jumping-spider thing again. Max slings him over his shoulder and heads for Seamus who's already in their regular booth.

Seamus, also a *Dottore*, says, 'Hi.'

'Heavy lifting,' says Max.

'Best avoided,' says Seamus.

Max wonders if he can get the dwarf off his shoulder and on to the seat between himself and the wall. He can, with the dwarf asleep again and snoring quietly. Max sighs, sits down, takes the two videos he's returning to Seamus out of his rucksack and puts them on the table. Seamus puts out three that Max lent him: *Field of Dreams*, *The Devil's Backbone*, and *The Princess and the Warrior*. Juliano brings them each a half-pint of lager and as they clink glasses Seamus says, 'Absent friends.'

'Why'd you say that?' says Max.

'Who knows?' says Seamus. 'There are bound to be some out there.'

'How's work?' says Seamus. 'Page One?'

'Not yet,' says Max. 'What about you? Episode Four?'

'Slow going,' says Seamus.

'Gentlemen?' says Juliano.

'Scampi,' say Max and Seamus.

'Problems?' says Max to Seamus.

Seamus nods. 'Gwendoline's realer than Daniel.'

'Women are realer than men,' says Max.

'You've noticed,' says Seamus as Juliano reappears with two more lagers.

'Are we hearing or have we heard music?' says Max's mind.

'What music?' says Max.

'What they usually have here,' says Seamus. 'Right now it's Georgy Zamfir and his pan pipes.'

'Sorry,' says Max. 'What did you say?'

'"Be not afeard,"' says Seamus; '"the isle is full of noises,/ Sounds and sweet airs that give delight and hurt not./ Sometimes a thousand twangling instruments/ Will hum about mine ears . . ."'

Juliano brings the scampi. Seamus says, 'You on for our usual video debauch at Virgin?'

'Not today,' says Max. 'Got to get back to my desk so I'm there in case Page One happens.'

'Was it yesterday, the music?' says his mind.

'I'll get back to you, OK?' says Max.

'About what?' says Seamus.

'Sorry,' says Max. 'Thinking out loud.'

Nobody has much to say after that. It's Max's turn to settle the bill. He does this and heaves the still-sleeping dwarf on to his shoulder. When they part Seamus wishes Max luck with the new novel and Max wishes Seamus luck with his *Daniel Deronda* for Radio 3. Then Seamus heads for Tottenham Court Road and the Virgin Megastore in Oxford Street while Max walks back to the Russell Square tube station and the Piccadilly Line. In the train Max remembers not to think out loud. People look at him and move away anyhow. 'What music are we talking about?' he says to his mind.

'Hang on,' says his mind. 'I'm giving you a picture.'

Max sees the doormat at home with its accumulation of flyers and cards for car services. Also something square and white. No, something *round* and white in a clear plastic square envelope.

'Now I'm thinking South Ken,' says his mind. 'I'm thinking V & A.'

'What about the doormat?' says Max.

'Later,' says his mind. 'First the V & A.'

The dwarf is asleep on Max's shoulder. Max can't see his face. He says to his mind, 'Hallucinations are mental things, right?'

'OK,' says his mind, 'but I didn't think this guy up. I'm

like a post office – things come in and I sort them. What stop is this?'

'Earls Court,' says Max.

'We missed South Ken!' says his mind. 'Go back.'

Max crosses to the eastbound Piccadilly platform and after about five minutes there's a train. It's crowded but people leave a little space around Max. Can they smell the dwarf? Max tries to look as if he doesn't care. The dwarf is awake now and singing softly to himself.

'What stop is this?' says his mind.

'Oh shit,' says Max. 'Knightsbridge.' He leaves the train and lugs his burden to the westbound platform again. 'Don't talk to me this time,' he says to his mind as he boards another train.

'I didn't talk last time,' says his mind.

'No more singing,' says Max to the dwarf. The dwarf stops singing but hums to himself.

'Where are we?' says Max's mind.

'Earls Court,' says Max. 'Missed South Ken again. I don't believe this.' He and his mind and the dwarf go up to the street and after a quarter of an hour Max gets a taxi. 'Can you take us to the V & A, please,' he says to the driver.

The driver looks around. 'How many are you?' he says.

'It's just me,' says Max. He grunts as he shifts the dwarf and heaves him on to the seat.

'I know how it is, mate,' says the driver. 'I've got back trouble too.'

'Dwarves happen,' says Max.

'You what?' says the driver.

'Shit happens,' says Max.

'Tell me about it,' says the driver. 'But at least the Gunners are doing better than they were.'

'I don't really follow football,' says Max.

'How long you here for?' says the driver.

'I live here.'

'How long?'

'Fifteen years.'

'What made you come here?'

'Oliver Onions.'

'Who's he?'

'A writer. Dead now. Wrote a ghost story called "The Beckoning Fair One".'

'You a writer too?' says the driver.

'Yes.'

'You ever seen a ghost?'

'Not exactly,' says Max. 'You?'

'In a way,' says the driver, 'you're sitting next to one.'

'What do you mean?' says Max. The dwarf is on his left. He doesn't see anyone on his right.

'Like the echo of a person,' says the driver. 'An echo you can see.'

'Can you see it now?'

'No, but if there's nobody in here with me and I look in the mirror I like get the idea of her face.'

'Someone you knew?'

'No, she was just a fare I picked up in the Fulham Road. Her and a bloke, they were going to Waterloo. I had the divider closed so I couldn't hear what they were saying but she was crying and shaking her head. She was a good-looking woman, very fine-featured, nothing common. Kept shaking her head and dabbing at her eyes with a handkerchief. The man, I didn't like the way his mouth moved and his hands. Didn't like his tie. The fare was nine pound twenty and he gave me eleven quid but I still didn't like him. They had one small bag, I think it was hers.'

'What do you think was making her cry?' says Max.

'I think he was telling her it was all over. I'd say she was better off without him but I can still see her crying and shaking her head. Here we are.'

The fare is five sixty. Max tips the driver eighty-five pence. 'The stories I could tell you!' says the driver. 'But I'm no good at writing them down.'

'Maybe they don't need to be written down,' says Max. 'Not everything does.' As the taxi pulls away into the traffic Max shoulders his dwarf and looks up and down the Cromwell Road. The evening sky is a darkening dove-grey still luminous with a Caspar David Friedrich long, long blue that is like memory, like prayer, like regret. There is a little sickle moon, Max is never sure whether it's waxing or waning. Against the sky the rooftops and chimneys, TV aerials and satellite dishes are like black paper silhouettes. Below the scissored-out black shapes are golden windows, orangey-yellow street lamps, the brilliant reds, green, and ambers of traffic lights, and the white headlights coming and red tail-lights going townward and homeward. The pattering of footsteps on the pavement makes him think of the wheeling of starlings, so many of them and name-less to him.

Up the steps he goes, through the revolving door and into the warmth and brightness of the Victoria and Albert Museum. Long spaces and echoes, years overlapped like fish scales. Bowls and goblets, wine of shadows. Women, men, gods and demons in stone, clay, bronze, ivory, some with open eyes, some with closed. Fabrics and jewels embracing absent friends.

'Nehru Gallery,' says Max's mind.

All of a sudden Max feels a strange lightness and he realises that the dwarf is gone.

'Don't let's celebrate yet,' says his mind. 'He'll probably be back.'

There are people all around with their voices and their footsteps and their cameras popping sudden flashes but Max feels all alone as he approaches the Nehru Gallery. Soon it will be Devali, and women in yellow, orange, red and purple saris trickle grains of coloured powders on to the floor in a likeness of Ganesha. 'Listen to the music,' says Max's mind. On a dais musicians with sitar, tabla, flute and harmonium are playing a classical raga, faraway warm and bright in the dark London November. The music is not loud but it is very wide. Max is standing in front of a display case in which he sees Shiva Nataraja dancing in bronze, his hair streaming symmetrically to right and left. Dancing in a bronze ring of fire, Shiva Nataraja with his four arms, his hands with drum, with flame, with 'Fear not', with pointing to his uplifted left foot. Under his right foot is a dwarf all blackish-green with patina. It has a long body, short arms and legs. Under Shiva's foot it is like an animal, something that goes on all fours. Its baby-face, is it reposeful? Max thinks it is. 'That's Apasmara Purusha,' says his mind. 'The dwarf demon called Forgetfulness.'

'Among other things,' says Max. 'And that's the guy I've been carrying around. Why'd he hop it all of a sudden?'

'He knew you'd recognise him if you looked at the bronze Apasmara and he was hoping to delay it,' says his mind. 'That's why he made us miss South Ken three times. He's not all that clever, actually.'

'He's not coming from you or me,' says Max. 'He's from somewhere else. Somebody put him on to me. Who?'

'What was that on the doormat?' says his mind.

'It was a CD,' says Max. 'The recordable kind.'

'From where? From whom?'

'Don't know,' says Max. 'No writing on it. Somebody'd pushed it through the letterbox.'

'We listened to it, didn't we?' says his mind. 'That's how this whole thing started.'

'You're right,' says Max.

'What was it?' says his mind.

Max closes his eyes, trying to remember. Almost he can hear it coming through the raga the musicians are playing but not quite. 'It was a raga,' he says.

'Let's go home,' says his mind.

2

AMAZING GRACE

November 2001. Max knows a little bit about a lot of things. He's read enough Hindu mythology to recall that Apasmara is Forgetfulness, Heedlessness, Selfishness, Ignorance, and Materialism. Those are some of his names but he could also be called Pain-in-the-Arse or Whatever-You-Don't-Want or The-One-Who-Doesn't-Return-Your-Calls or any other hard name you can think of. *Somebody's* got to be under Shiva's right foot and he's it. Maybe he likes it there, who knows? In bronze he'll stay under Shiva's foot, but in reality he's a freelance demon and he'll go wherever he's sent. So who sent him to Max?

Nothing bad happens on the way home from the V & A but Max keeps looking around like a hunted man and people give him plenty of space in the tube. Several men are watching him closely, ready to jump him if he turns out to be a suicide bomber.

'Everybody can see there's something wrong with me,' says Max to his mind.

'Steady, boy,' says his mind. 'Stay with me, I'll get you through this.'

Max gets home safely and pours himself a large Glenfiddich.

'What we should do now,' says his mind, 'is get some expert advice.'

'Where?' says Max.

'Remember Istvan Fallok, Hermes Soundways?'

'What a good idea,' says Max. He knocks back another large Glenfiddich, puts the CD in his pocket and a fresh bottle in his shoulder bag, and he's off.

By the time he comes out of the Bakerloo Line at Oxford Circus it's night-time. The sky that was clear over South Kensington has clouded up and is gently raining. The glistening streets are alive with reflected lights of all colours, even words and names. The hiss of tyres on the wet whispers that you never know what might happen next. Feeling like a doomed hero in his own movie, Max goes by way of Argyll Street, Great Marlborough, Carnaby and Marshall to Broadwick, then to an enclave of small businesses and light manufacturing off Broadwick. Places that look like message drops for secret agents while producing pens with your name and address on them and novelty key rings. Hermes Soundways is a little twilit studio down a flight of iron steps that ping and patter as the rain hardens up.

By now it's after seven but business hours mean nothing to Istvan Fallok. He's a twenty-four-hour person who probably sleeps somewhere sometime but not noticeably. His Soho lair is full of tiny winking red, yellow, and green eyes. Green waves oscillate and blue bars leap up and down on various screens. From speakers as big as fridges issues the sound of a sitar. 'Favourable sign, that,' says Max's mind. Rising from the depths like the Kraken is Fallok, fifty-nine, tall, pale, his red hair flecked with grey. He knows all there is to know about sound and he knows Max because he did the track for a short film Max wrote a couple of years ago, *If I Forget Thee*.

13

'Hi,' says Max. 'Remember me?'

'Max Lesser,' says Fallok. 'You look anxious. What can I do for you today?'

Max offers the bottle of Glenfiddich. Fallok finds two cloudy glasses, opens the bottle, pours a drink for each of them, clinks with Max, sips, sighs, and leans back in his swivel chair. 'You have my ear,' he says. 'For a limited time.'

'I've got a problem you might be able to help me with,' says Max. 'What's that on your speakers?'

'*Adana.*'

'It sounds like a 'round-midnight kind of raga.'

'It is. That's because around here it's always around midnight. You into Indian music?'

'I listen to it sometimes but I don't know much about it. Somebody sent me a CD with a raga on it and it did something to my head.'

'What?'

Max tells Fallok about the whole Apasmara business and they both have another drink. 'Got the CD with you?' says Fallok. He ejects *Adana* from the player.

'Why are you crying?' says Max.

'I'm not crying,' says Fallok with tears streaming down his face.

'Aren't you going to play my CD?' says Max.

'I just did,' says Fallok. 'Where were you?'

'Don't know,' says Max. 'So what can you tell me? What did you hear in that music?'

Fallok shakes his head as if he's trying to clear it. 'I don't remember,' he says. He touches his cheek. 'OK, maybe I was crying. So obviously the music hooked up with something in me. Music does that, it feeds that which it findeth. If it made

14

you see Apasmara it's because he was already hanging around somewhere in your mind.'

'And that's all you can tell me?'

'That's all. It's that kind of thing.'

'That's a wonderful diagnosis,' says Max. 'But how do I get him off me?'

'Is he on you now?'

'No, but I know he'll be back.'

'Nothing I can do about that,' says Fallok. 'You let him in and you'll have to find a way to get him out. Any idea who'd want to put Apasmara on to you?'

'Nope,' says Max as his mind comes up empty.

'Well,' says Fallok, 'I'm sorry I can't be more helpful but I have to get back to work now.'

'What do I owe you?' says Max.

'This one's on the house. Thanks for the whisky and good luck. Here, don't forget your CD.'

Max doesn't want to leave, doesn't want to be alone with himself. 'I don't know where to turn next,' he says.

Fallok sighs. From the clutter on his workbench he takes a business card: *All That Glisters*, **Grace Kowalski**. It's in Berwick Street. 'Here,' he says, 'I'll call her and tell her you're coming. She lives over the shop.'

'What is she?' says Max.

'Unusual. She might be able to help you. She likes vodka. Off you go.'

All That Glisters has a good sound to Max and now the rain cheers him up. Berwick Street is quite close, and on the way he buys a bottle of Stolichnaya. It looks so clear and promising that he buys a second one, he wants to show willing. Berwick Street is crowded with shops and already he feels less alone. All That Glisters has a window full of interesting and expensive jewellery. It feels lucky to Max. The shop is dimly lit but the studio above it looks wide awake. Max rings the bell, hears footsteps on the stairs, the door opens and Grace Kowalski appears. She's tall, gaunt, early forties maybe, dark circles under her eyes. Long black hair parted on the side and hanging straight down. Blue denim shirt not tucked in, jeans, bare feet, long and shapely.

'Hi,' she says. 'Istvan phoned me about you.' They shake hands. She has a good grip. 'Come up,' she says. 'I just have a little bit of work to finish, then we can talk about what's happening with you.'

Once in the studio, Max gives her the vodka. 'Thank you,' she says. '*Two* bottles!'

'Belt and braces,' says Max as she finds two glasses and pours for them both.

'Here's to form and emptiness,' she says.

'Whichever,' says Max.

Grace takes her drink to her workbench which is in a corner of the room. It's littered with tools, rolls of wire, and boxes of sparkly things lit by an Anglepoise lamp. There's a salty sulphurous smell mixed with the smoke of her last cigarette as she makes herself a Golden Virginia roll-up and offers the tobacco and papers to Max. He declines. She lights up and gets back to work on the brooch she's finishing. It's a figure set with red and blue and yellow stones.

'The Hanged Man,' says Max. Grace shows him the card she's working from, XXII *Le Pendu* in the Marseilles Tarot. 'Very popular,' she says. 'We're all of us in suspension.'

'Do you believe in the Tarot?' says Max.

'I don't believe in anything,' says Grace. 'You?'

'I believe in this dwarf I've been carrying around.'

'We'll get to him in a moment,' says Grace. 'Bear with me.'

She's been using tweezers very delicately. 'There,' she says, and puts the tweezers down. 'It's finished.' She leans back, rolls another cigarette, lights up, and refills their glasses.

'It looks good,' says Max.

'It better, I'm going to get a lot of money for it. I have a select clientele for this kind of thing: Tarot, Zodiac, I Ching.' She moves gracefully off the chair and sits on the floor almost in a lotus position. 'Join me,' she says, 'and tell me what's happening.'

Max gets down on the floor (non-lotus) and tells her everything. 'Do you want to listen to the CD?' he says.

'I don't need it,' says Grace. I'll be working from your end. I have this one thing I can do. Maybe it'll help, maybe not. First listen to this.' She takes a folded piece of paper from her shirt pocket and reads:

'Here, O Sariputra. Form is emptiness and the very emptiness is form; emptiness does not differ from form, form does not differ from emptiness; whatever is form, that is emptiness, whatever is emptiness, that is form, the same is true of feelings, perceptions, impulses and consciousness.

How does that grab you?'

'Works for me,' says Max. 'Are you a Buddhist?'

'I'm not anything but if form and emptiness are the same then so are Buddhism and non-Buddhism and the Heart Sutra should work for me, which it does. I've never even read the whole thing. Istvan showed me the book and that part leapt out at me. All of a sudden my head seemed to open up in all directions and I knew I could do it.'

'Do what?'

'Get with the form of emptiness and the emptiness of form.'

Maybe it's her voice, maybe it's the words, maybe it's the whisky and vodka on an empty stomach: Max feels as if he's far away and high up, standing on the edge of something. Grace's haggard face, the light of the lamp, the tools and things on the workbench, the smell of the place – maybe they'll stop being there.

'Don't look down,' says his mind.

'How do you do it?' says Max to Grace.

'I just let myself be with it, and I can get you to be with it if you want. Do you want to do it?'

'Yes,' says Max.

'OK,' says Grace. 'Close your eyes and we'll both say the name of Apasmara until you see the form of him. It could take a while but we'll do it until he shows up. When you see him I'll see him too. Then we change his name a little to deny him recognition. We'll call him Napasmara until his emptiness appears. When that happens maybe we'll see where he's coming from. This'll take a lot of juice from both of us, so move your mind away from all interference and let the energy rise up in you.' Grace's voice is low and husky. Her words enter Max as if she's a priestess and he obeys. His mind becomes clear and immensely deep as the energy rises up in him.

'Apasmara,' he says. Grace is saying it with him, he can feel her voice becoming big and far away, his own with it. They sound like the vocal chording of Tibetan monks. 'Apasmara!' How many times have they said it? Max feels himself moving slowly apart as the room disappears. After a long time here is the huddled form of the dwarf demon. Apasmara writhing and glaring with burning eyes. Apasmara hissing and spitting with the rage that's in him.

'Napasmara!' Grace and Max and others chant hugely.

What others – absent friends? 'Napasmara!' Again and again they voice the name that denies the form of the dwarf. It seems hours before he begins to scatter like ashes in the wind as emptiness enters him. Apasmara has become not there. Now there is a fresh dimness like the mist over a waterfall, moving aside to disclose blue eyes, direct and unfathomable. Now appears a woman's face with chiselled features, sweet mouth, rose-petal lips, delicate pink tongue. 'Lola!' whispers Max. 'Lola Bessington!' Ridiculously, he finds himself singing:

> 'Her name was Lola, she was a showgirl,
> With yellow feathers in her hair
> And her dress cut down to there . . .'

'Lola!' says Max. 'I didn't even remember that she was gone until just now. Not only is she gone, she's even sent Apasmara to take away all memory of her.' Sitting on the floor, he hugs his knees and rocks back and forth, weeping.

3

WHEN MAX MET LOLA

December 1996. Lola Bessington was beautiful but she was not a showgirl. When Max met her it was cold and crisp, the air sharp with Christmas. Pavements bulging with burdened shoppers. Fretful eyes, rosy cheeks, clouds of breath. Doorways fully staffed with homeless. Max comes through Cecil Court, crosses St Martin's Lane, passes the Coliseum entrance, goes into the Coliseum Shop. It's bright and warm and festive, buzzing with customers doing their bit for the economy. Lola's reaching up to get something off the shelves for a customer. Short skirts! Max's heart leaps like a salmon jumping a waterfall. The music on the speakers is Monteverdi's *L'Orfeo*. A good omen, he thinks. That's the opera he's come here to buy.

He follows Lola and her customer back to the counter. She has elegant legs and Max knows instinctively that her mind is equally elegant. While he waits his turn he hears *L'Orfeo* as if for the first time. His thoughts about Lola have naturally been carnal, he's hard-wired for that, but now the music is getting to him. As Lola completes the sale he notes that her eyes are blue, direct and unfathomable. Her voice is a clear stream in a dappled wood, her accent is patrician. 'If I can have her,' he thinks, 'my love will never die.'

'Hi,' says Lola. 'Can I help you?' The salary she earns in the shop just about pays for taxis and lunches but it gives her a feeling of independence. Her father is the Rt. Hon. Lord Bessington, Lord of Appeal in Ordinary. Lady Bessington is on the Board of Trustees of the Royal Opera. Lola lives with them in a big house in Belgravia and the Bessingtons also own a villa in Tuscany. Lola's been to Roedean and Cambridge where she got a first in Anthropology. Max's situation, some might say, is not unlike that of a minor-league baseball player hoping to get to the big show.

Lola, twenty-five, has had a few inconsequential romances in her first years at Cambridge and in her last year she met Basil Meissen-Potts. He was like a specimen out of a Mr Right catalogue. At thirty-five, he was a QC and very silky. Tall, handsome, charming, good sense of humour, a judo black belt, an accomplished cricketer and keen yachtsman. Lola's parents look on the couple as practically engaged. Lola doesn't quite. Two things are against him: one, Mummy and Daddy approve of him; two, he's never really lit Lola's fire.

'Hi,' says Max. 'Whose recording of *L'Orfeo* am I hearing?'

'John Eliot Gardiner, conducting the Monteverdi Choir, the English Baroque Soloists, His Majesties Sagbutts and Cornetts,' says Lola. 'What do you think?'

'I'll have it,' says Max. He already owns that recording but he follows Lola to the shelf where Monteverdi lives. She hands him the Archiv boxed set of two CDs.

'I have a thing for sagbutts and cornetts,' she says.

'Me too,' says Max. 'What's your name?'

'Lola.' (When Max doesn't sing the Barry Manilow song

he scores a couple of points.) 'I love Monteverdi,' she says. 'He breaks your heart in a very unsentimental way.'

'I have a lot of time for Monteverdi,' says Max. He hasn't listened to Monteverdi for about a year and a half. He's in the shop now because he wants a new copy of *L'Orfeo* for the novel he's trying to start. It's a superstition thing.

'He's not too realistic, if you know what I mean,' says Lola. 'He's like Giotto or . . .'

'Lorenzetti?' says Max.

'When's Lorenzetti?'

'Fourteenth century,' says Max. 'He did some allegorical frescoes in a *palazzo* in Siena. Very formal, somewhat stilted but in a lively way. Real but not too real.'

'That's it,' says Lola. Now she's really seeing Max with those blue eyes. He's nothing special to look at but he knows what she means when she talks about not too realistic. 'Have you got *L'incoronazione di Poppea*?' Max loves the way the title rolls off her tongue.

'Yes,' he says. 'It's quite an old recording, the one with Nikolaus Harnoncourt and the Concentus Musicus Wien. I bought it after a Glyndebourne production at Sadler's Wells. I wanted to hear Ottavia sing "*A Dio, Roma*" again.'

'You won't believe this,' says Lola. 'I have the same recording and I bought it after going to that same production. Maybe we were there on the same night.' Does she know that she's lighting Max's touchpaper?

Whoosh! High in the sky goes Rocket Max. Showers of stars explode over the Coliseum, it's like a movie. The stick falls back to earth in St Martin's Lane. 'This is it,' he says to his mind. 'This is the real thing. This is my destiny woman.' All through the shop heads turn. 'Did I say that out loud?' he says.

'Audibly,' says Lola. Blushing.

'What do I do now?' says Max.

'Pay for the recording,' she says. Safely behind the counter she takes Max's American Express card. Seeing his name she says, 'Are you the Max Lesser who wrote *Any That You Can Not Put Downe?*'

'That's me,' says Max. 'Don't tell me you've read it?'

'It kept me up half the night,' says Lola. 'I love spooky stories.' She bags the Monteverdi, smiles, says, 'See you,' turns to the next in the queue, says, 'Yes, please?'

'Love!' says Max to his mind as they go out into the cold again. 'I kept her up half the night and she said "love".'

'Spooky stories,' says his mind.

'Love,' says Max. 'She said she'd see me.' He picks up the fallen rocket stick, hugs it to his bosom.

4

THROUGH THE NIGHT

That was December 1996. This is November 2001. Grace and Max sit on the floor for a long time without a word. Finally Grace says, 'I hope that put something into you, because it sure as hell took something out of me.'

'How could I have forgotten Lola?' says Max.

'Evidently that's the kind of thing Apasmara does,' says Grace.

'And then, out of nowhere, her face,' says Max. 'I'm trying to get my head around what happened.'

'First we saw the form of Apasmara,' says Grace. 'Then we saw the emptiness of him.'

'And then we saw Lola because she's the one who filled up his emptiness and sent him on to me,' says Max. 'From where? Where is she? I haven't been able to locate her for the last four years.'

'I can't help you with where she is,' says Grace.

'And why would she send a dwarf demon to make me forget her? Why *now*?'

'Can you reach the vodka?' says Grace.

On his hands and knees Max fetches both bottles. 'Here's looking at you,' he says as they kill the first bottle. 'You done good, Grace, and me a stranger.'

'We're all strangers,' says Grace through a cloud of Golden Virginia smoke, 'and you don't know what anyone is to you until they're gone. She was very beautiful.'

'She was a lot more than that,' says Max. 'She still is.'

With a half-shake of her head Grace makes a sympathetic sound, 'Tsst.'

Max looks at his watch. 'Jesus,' he says, 'it's twenty past three. I think it was only about half-past nine when I got here.'

'Form and emptiness take a while,' says Grace.

'I wonder if I'll sleep tonight,' says Max. 'There's no telling when Apasmara's going to turn up again, and this time he'll be madder than hell. But I can hardly keep my eyes open.'

'You'd better sleep here,' says Grace, 'Apasmara won't bother you while you're with me.'

'Thanks, I could crash right here on the floor.'

'You'll feel better waking up in a bed,' says Grace, and leads the way to the bedroom. There's a big bed but that's all there is to sleep on.

'You want us to sleep together?' says Max.

'Just sleep,' says Grace. 'Just to make it through the night.'

'Do you have bad nights?' says Max.

'I have all kinds of things,' says Grace. She goes into the bathroom, comes out in a long T-shirt with an I Ching hexagram on it.

'Which one is that?' says Max.

'Difficulty at the Beginning.'

'What about the middle?'

'I haven't got that far yet.' She slides into bed.

Max goes to the bathroom, pees, washes his face, rinses his mouth. He comes back to the bedroom, undresses down to

25

his underwear, hangs his clothes over a chair, and slides in beside Grace but not too close.

Grace is lying on her side with her back to him. He lies down facing the same way. She moves closer until her back is against his front and she takes his arm and brings it over her waist. 'I'm not making a pass,' she says. 'It's a comfort thing.'

'I know how it is,' says Max. He feels her ribs through the T-shirt as she snuggles against him and sighs like a sleepy child. 'Good night, Grace.'

'Night, Max.'

'So frail,' says Max's mind, 'but Apasmara's afraid of her.'

'She knows form and she knows emptiness,' says Max.

'Maybe you can learn that.'

'I'm not sure it's something you can learn,' says Max.

He hears birds singing. Maybe he's already asleep and dreaming. In the dream he's with Lola in Dorset four years ago. It's the afternoon of 21 March and they're on Maiden Castle with a picnic hamper and three bottles of champagne that she's brought. The day is bright and sunny but on the cool side and there's a fresh breeze blowing on top of the ancient hill fort. 'Absent friends,' says Lola as she pours a little Cristal on the ground. She takes the ribbon from her hair, ties it to a long stem of grass where it flutters like a tiny banner. 'They're all around us,' she says.

'All around us,' says Max. He notices Noah's Ark stranded on the hill fort not far from where he and Lola are sitting. A window near the roof opens and a raven flies out, loops the loop and is gone as Max wakes up and forgets the dream. Grace is warm against him, snoring gently. Birds are singing in Berwick Street, it's light outside.

Grace opens her eyes. 'I had a really good night,' she says. 'Thank you, Max.'

'It's for me to thank you,' says Max. A brief hug, then they get dressed and Grace shows Max where things are in the kitchen.

'You make the coffee,' says Grace. 'I'll get us some bagels.'

'Let me go for the bagels,' says Max.

'No,' says Grace. 'I like going out and knowing that I'm not coming back to an empty flat.'

Max has the coffee ready when she returns and they have a quiet breakfast. 'Well,' he says, 'I can't hide out here indefinitely. It's time for me to go out into the world again. I owe you, Grace.'

'Any time. Don't be a stranger.'

They part with a big hug and a small kiss and Max is on his own again.

5

FROM WHERE, FROM WHAT

November 2001. Max is afraid that Apasmara will destroy him. And of course it's Max's fear that gives Apasmara that power. What did Max do that made Apasmara come to him with Lola's music? Before we get into that we need to know something about where Max is coming from.

Now in 2001 Max is forty-four. So when he met Lola he was thirty-nine. Unmarried. What, had he never up till then found the right woman? Who can say what makes a woman the right one? Who can say what makes a person move forward or step back?

People are composed of memories, losses, longings and regrets. Max's father, now dead, lost a favourite toy as a child: a Noah's Ark. 'Noah and Mrs Noah and all the animals were printed on glossy paper that was glued to their plywood shapes,' he told Max. 'The Ark itself was yellow with a red roof. Did I play with it down in the cellar? I'm not sure. In the winter it was always warm and cosy there from the coal furnace. I liked the smell of it. There was a big black boiler by the opposite wall, it was a lying-down thing with big rivets. I used to think the Noah's Ark had fallen behind it somehow – there was just enough space between it and the wall. There were cables and pipes and cobwebs and I could never make anything out with a flashlight or find it with a stick. I didn't like to reach in with my hand because I was pretty sure there were spiders. By now the glossy paper would be all black with mildew but even now, in this house, I still want to look behind the boiler now and then.' Max remembers how his father sounded when he told that story.

Max has been in love many times with women who loved him back but he always fell out of love after a while. Constancy has not been his strong suit. In all fairness he ought to have been wearing a sign that said, IT AIN'T NECESSARILY SO when he appeared in the Coliseum Shop in 1996 and said that Lola was his destiny woman. None the less he was being perfectly honest: he believed it *was* necessarily so. He had truly fallen in love (in his way) and when he presented himself as an idea whose time had come, he was doing it in good faith.

Lola was too sensible to take Max's outburst any more seriously than the sort of shout she might hear when passing a building site. But at the same time something in her responded to his craziness. Mummy and Daddy and Basil were boringly sane while this man definitely had a screw loose which was not without its appeal. And his non-crazy remarks about Monteverdi and Lorenzetti showed him to have the kind of mind she was very comfortable with. For the rest of that evening she found herself replaying his declaration in her head. She was certain he'd show up again and she wondered what she'd do. She tried to imagine presenting Max to her parents. Lesser was almost certainly a Jewish name, and although one or two of Daddy's Jewish colleagues had dined at the house, there were none that he played golf with. Her mother had sometimes entertained Jewish singers and musicians but that was nothing that created problems. As Max was an artist, it wouldn't be like bringing a pawnbroker home but questions would be asked, with amiable interest, about Max's origins and education. At that point in her imaginings Lola gave herself a mental shake and resolved not to think too much about Max. She did, however, look for him in *Who's Who*. He wasn't there.

6

FIRST DATE

December 1996. Three days after his first appearance at the Coliseum Shop Max turns up again. This time he doesn't embarrass Lola and his visit is very brief. There'll be a performance of a new arrangement of *Die Winterreise* at Queen Elizabeth Hall in January. Would she like to go with him? She would. While pretending to help him look for a recording she gives him her last name and they exchange phone numbers. His mind spins like a prayer wheel, saying 'Lola Bessington' all the way home.

Over Christmas and New Year Max drinks more than his usual quota. He watches war films on TV in which the Germans speak heavily accented English and the Allied soldiers speak German like natives while infiltrating the enemy. He also draws heavily on the resources of Blockbuster. He works every day, trying for a new story in his children's series about a hedgehog called Charlotte Prickles.

January 1997. On the appointed evening Max meets Lola at the shop at half-past six and they walk to the Embankment and over the Hungerford Bridge to the South Bank. On the bridge they both give money to the homeless and feel guilty because they feel so good. Halfway across, Lola turns to look up at Ursa Major low in the sky over Charing Cross Station. She knows the names of the seven stars of that constellation but on the first date she's not ready to say them for Max who is also looking up. To him Ursa Major is the Big Dipper and the dipper is upright. 'Nothing has spilt out yet,' he says.

Lola smiles and says nothing. She feels good about Max. She likes being with him, and his choice of *Die Winterreise* was a good one. Comfortably sheltered in Belgravia and cherished by Daddy, Mummy, and Basil, she feels herself to be all alone, a solitary wayfarer on a journey to nowhere, past barking dogs and windows warm in the cold night.

'What made you decide on Schubert for tonight?' she asks Max.

'The man in *Die Winterreise* says that he came as a stranger and he goes as a stranger,' says Max. 'That's how I've always felt.'

'Me too,' says Lola. 'Do you know anything about this performance?'

'It's the first time in London and it's billed as some kind of synthesis with orchestra and tenor. The composer is Hans Zender, the tenor is Christoph Pregardien, and the orchestra is the Klangforum Wien under Sylvain Gambreling. I haven't heard of any of them before.'

They give money again at the South Bank end of the bridge and have time for coffee in the Queen Elizabeth Hall cafeteria. Max and Lola both look around at the other people, smug in the knowledge that they're on the inside of something that everybody else is on the outside of. The other coffee-drinkers look as if they mostly read the *Guardian* and the *Independent* and quite a few of them seem to know each other.

Once inside, Max and Lola settle comfortably into their

seats and wait for the Schubert to happen. Accustomed to this song cycle performed by two men and one piano, both of them are slightly startled by the sight of instrumentalists. 'It'll be *Die Winterreise*, but not as we know it,' says Max.

'I tend to be a traditionalist,' says Lola, 'but I'm always interested in new approaches.'

Sylvain Gambreling appears, waves his musicians to their feet. He and they bow together and are applauded. Christoph Pregardien takes the stage, bows, is applauded, the orchestra tunes up, and they're off. Some of the musicians are active with their instruments but whatever they're doing is almost inaudible. Pregardien isn't opening his mouth. Very, very gradually one hears something like the beating of a heart coming closer, closer. Is that the melody of the first song, '*Gute Nacht*,' sneaking in behind that heartbeat, like the voice of the singer trying to find him?

Louder now, with strings, percussion, brass, woodwinds, the heartbeat, footsteps perhaps, now near, now far. Loud, loud suddenly, a summons from the horns. Max's and Lola's hands find each other. Is there, they wonder, a madness that we inhabit and call reality? Is this music letting it in? Was this always in Schubert, waiting to be called up? When will the singer be heard? Now at last, gently with strings the melody of '*Gute Nacht*', and now the voice of Christoph Pregardien: '*Fremd bin ich eingezogen, Fremd zieh ich wieder aus*'; 'A stranger I came, a stranger I go again'. That voice! Pure, ingenuous, going straight to the heart more than Fischer-Dieskau, more than any other tenor that Max and Lola have ever heard. Tears are running down Lola's face, Max's also. He squeezes her hand, she squeezes back.

7

SO FAR, SO SOON

January 1997. Zender's *Die Winterreise* goes on with all kinds of surprises, loud and soft, shouted, brassed, stringed, clanged and thumped. Pregardien's singing is a revelation. But the main event of the evening is the crying. Ending up in bed with Max this night would not shock Lola. But to cry together? She hasn't been prepared for that degree of intimacy on the first date. On the way back over the Hungerford Bridge both she and Max look up at Ursa Major. This time she too thinks of it as the Big Dipper. Now it's standing on its handle, so that whatever was in it has poured out. Is Max already someone to be seriously reckoned with? Despite youthful romances Lola has never given her heart completely and for ever. If she finds herself at the edge of This-Is-It she won't be afraid to leap. Is that edge getting closer?

8

RAZOR BLADES

Now we're back in November 2001. Max is on his way home from Grace Kowalski's as the memory of that first date bursts into his head ten times more vivid than it was before Apasmara took it away. And it hurts. It hurts like a head full of double-edged razor blades. 'Shit!' says Max as he realises that Apasmara's thing isn't only forgetfulness – it's whatever hurts the most.

'Oi!' comes a loathsome whisper behind him. 'Have I got to writhe all the way back to Fulham or are you going to take me aboard?' There he is in his run-over-dog mode.

'Get lost, Napasmara,' says Max. 'You're nothing but a whole lot of emptiness.'

'That makes two of us then,' says the dwarf, 'because I'm whatever you are and that denial shit only works when you're with Kowalski. Come on, pick me up. I ain't heavy, I'm your brother.'

So Max picks him up. Apasmara's weight and smell are just as bad as before but somehow Max feels more . . . what? More *complete* with the dwarf demon on his back as they near Oxford Circus. 'I suppose,' says his mind, 'it's better to have him inside the tent pissing out than outside pissing in.'

'Except that he's inside pissing in,' says Max.

'Anyhow, I'm getting used to it,' says his mind. 'What an evening that first date was. What a memory. It hurts like hell but it's a beauty. Those stars over Charing Cross Station! The feel of Lola's hand squeezing yours!'

'Don't distract me,' says Max. 'I'm reviewing the situation. Lola put Apasmara on to me with this CD. Could she have been the one who put it through the letterbox?'

'You think she's still in London?' says his mind.

'Hang on,' says Max as WHAM, another memory lights up his brain: Trafalgar Square the Monday evening a couple of days after *Die Winterreise*. The Coliseum Shop closes at six on Mondays and it's only about half-past now. The National Gallery also closes at six so people from there have joined those already in the Square. Gentle rain coming down. Max and Lola in macs and broad-brimmed canvas hats, one of which Max bought for Lola this afternoon. 'Do you buy a lot of hats,' she says, 'for women?'

'First time,' says Max. 'I thought you might like to walk in the rain without an umbrella.'

'I do, and you got the size right too. Well done.' She's on his arm and the two of them are the little village of each other in the winter night. Under the lights and the rain the lions are gleaming, the fountains are sending up their white spray, the passing sightseeing buses are juicily red, and Nelson, as in all weathers, keeps watch from his column.

'I've been thinking about *Die Winterreise*,' says Lola.

'Me too,' says Max. 'Some of those songs seem to describe exactly where I am in my own *Reise*.'

'Same here,' says Lola. 'In that very first song, "*Gute Nacht*", the second verse keeps singing itself in my head. I did my own translation with the help of the Fischer-Dieskau CD text: "I

can to my journey not choose me the time. I must myself
the way find in this darkness. It goes a moon-shadow as my
companion. And in the white fields seek I the wild animals'
tracks." That got to me: "I can to my journey not choose
me the time."'

'Nobody can,' says Max.

'But what if you're not ready for the journey?'

'I think maybe nobody's ever ready for the big ones,'
says Max.

Lola says nothing, she presses closer to him.

'What a memory,' says Max's mind. 'But those razor
blades!'

'She's in London,' says Max. 'I can feel it.'

'What year are you in?'

'This one, right now.' He turns on his heel and heads for
Trafalgar Square.

9

FLASHES, FLUTTERS,
EXPECTATIONS

November 2001. Vibrating like a caesium clock, Max makes his way southeast through Soho. The years from 1996 onwards print his footsteps as he goes. From Berwick Street to Broadwick, Broadwick to Wardour, then across Shaftesbury to Whitcomb and Pall Mall East. Lola-and-Max phantasms beckon and lure as he passes places where they ate, drank, and dawdled. Max's thoughts pop like camera flashes and flutter like the pigeons of, here it is: Trafalgar Square.

England expects! shouts Nelson from his column.

'Me too,' says Max. So many footsteps, faces, seconds, minutes, hours, pigeons. Is she here? If not, why not? Multitudes of voices, wings, cameras. Was that Trafalgar Square memory a message from Lola or was it not? His chest feels wet. 'You pissed on me!' he says to Apasmara.

'It's all in your mind,' says the dwarf.

'I have no control over him,' says Max's mind.

'Why not?' says Max.

'Don't get heavy with me,' says his mind. 'We've got to stick together to get through this.'

'Sorry.'

'Maybe you're trying too hard. Maybe if you ease up a little . . .'

'If I ease up a little, what? Suddenly she'll appear and everything will be the way it was before it stopped being that way?'

'Stop straining for special effects, Max. Just go for ordinary memories with no frills.'

'Can we do straight memories now?' says Max, 'like regular people?'

'Let's try,' says his mind.

10

FRANK SINATRA, DORIS DAY

February 1997. The lights of the Albert Bridge are beads of
hope strung across the night. Max and Lola both have songs
in their heads: Max's song is the Frank Sinatra version of
'My One and Only Love'. Lola's is the Doris Day 'If I Give
My Heart to You'. They're both thinking a lot and not
talking much as they walk along the Embankment towards
the Chelsea Bridge. After a while Lola says, 'I think I should
tell you about Basil Meissen-Potts.'

'Fragile, is he?' says Max. In his mind stamping heavily
upon the Meissen-Pottsery of the unknown Basil.

'Not at all,' says Lola. 'He's a black belt and a demon
cricketer. His main thing is being a QC.'

'Why do you need to tell me about him?'

'Well, Daddy and Mummy rather expect me to marry him.
Not that I want to.'

'I should hope not.'

'All the same, he's part of a kind of life that I'm accustomed to,
and it isn't something one walks away from lightly. I'll follow my
heart wherever it takes me but it's got to be the real thing.' She
and Max have so far used the word *love* only in connection with
spooky stories, Monteverdi, rain, the Albert Bridge, and so on.

'Are you the real thing?' says Max's mind.

'How real can I be, for Christ's sake?' says Max. 'Some mornings when I wake up I'm not even there.'

'I wonder how long the light bulbs on the Albert Bridge last,' says Lola.

'They can always get new ones as the old ones burn out,' says Max. 'It'll never go dark.'

BLIGHTER'S ROCK NO

February 1997. When Max isn't with Lola and also when he is, he's looking for Page One. This is a bit like trying to retrieve a coin that's fallen down a grating. Is that it, that faint gleam in the darkness? Not sure. He lowers weighted strings and chewing gum and brings up bottle caps.

'Blighter's rock?' says Max's mind.

'I am not rocked,' says Max. He avoids the proper name of that condition in which writers are unable to write. 'My ideas aren't the usual thing and they don't come easy.' His last novel, *Any That You Can Not Put Downe*, published in 1993, was about a man's pursuit of the ghost of a woman who put a curse on him. His two previous novels, *Turn Down An Empty Glass* and *Ten Thousand Several Doors*, were published five and seven years ago respectively. For each of these Max received a twenty-thousand-pound advance. None of the three has yet earned back that advance. Fortunately *Charlotte Prickles, Lollipop Lady* was a commercial success when it came out in 1994, and his juvenile backlist is healthy. So Max can afford to write another novel. If he can think of one.

'I'm starting to get a kind of flavour,' says his mind.

'What kind of flavour?'

'Dark, shadowy, sad, full of loss.'

'I'm tasting it,' says Max. 'It's very disturbing.'

'But it's your kind of thing, no?'

'Yes, but it scares me.'

'Scared is good, isn't it?'

'Not this kind,' says Max. 'It's not the normal kind of writing panic. It's full of regret.'

'For what?'

'I don't know and I'm afraid to find out.'

12

WHEN CLAUDE MET
LULA MAE

February 1997. A Sunday afternoon. Max and Lola in the
National Gallery, standing in front of Claude's *Landscape with
Psyche outside of the Palace of Cupid*. 'Poor Psyche!' says Lola.

'If she hadn't lit that lamp to sneak a peek at Cupid he
wouldn't have flown away,' says Max. 'But she wasn't content
to be kept in the dark.'

'No one likes to be kept in the dark,' says Lola. 'Now
she's lost her love and there's darkness all around her.'

'Consequences of . . .' says Max. He's picking up a scent,
a fragrance.

'Of what?' says Lola.

'Magnolia blossoms?' says Max. He turns to see a young
woman looking at the same picture. A homecoming-queen
kind of beauty and he can tell by the hang of her face that
she's American.

'Clawed!' she says. 'You can't beat him for atmosphere.'

'Clowed,' says Max.

'But in *Casablanca* it's Clawed Rains who says, "Round up
the usual suspects,"' says the homecoming queen.

'In the National Gallery it's Clowed,' says Max.

44

'I'll keep that in mind. I'm Lula Mae Flowers.'

'Max Lesser.' Handshake. 'This is Lola Bessington.'

'Hi,' says Lula Mae to Lola. To Max she says, 'You here for a visit?'

'I live here. You?'

'I work here as of last week, Everest Technology Sales, transferred from Austin. What do you do?'

'Write,' says Max. 'Novels.'

'What have you written?'

'*Any That You Can Not Put Downe* was the most recent. Not published in the States.'

'You're an H. P. Lovecraft fan! How about that! So far from home!' She speaks with exclamation marks.

'I think I've seen enough of this one,' says Lola to Max. 'I'll move on to the next room.' To Lula Mae she says, 'Nice meeting you.'

'Likewise,' says Lula Mae.

'I hope you enjoy London,' says Max to her as he follows Lola.

'Do my best. Maybe our paths will cross again.'

'You never know,' says Max as he watches the sweet primeval motion of her going-away view.

'I never noticed till now that your eyes are on stalks,' says Lola.

'Retractable,' says Max.

'I think Lula Mae Magnolia Blossom has gone,' says Lola, 'and I want to get back to the Claweds.' She leads the way to *A Seaport with the Embarkation of the Queen of Sheba.* 'There's the ship waiting to take her away into the early morning with fair weather and favouring winds. It looks as if it's happening on a stage, I can almost hear the rollers creaking as the waves lap at the shore. How many filters of unreality are there between the real Queen of Sheba and this one!'

'Unreality is part of reality,' says Max.

13

WHEN MAX'S MIND MET
LULA MAE

February 1997. Still that Sunday. 'No,' says Max's mind.
'What no?' says Max.

'You're not going to have a go at that sweet primeval
motion.'

'You sound as if I have a go at anything that moves,'
says Max.

'So you won't be looking up Everest Technology in the
phone book?'

'Give me a break. She's a little bit of home, and naturally
if I bump into her we'll have a coffee or something.'

'A little bit of home! What, now you're from Texas?'

'You know what I mean.'

'I certainly do. Coffee or something! You've got a real
thing going with Lola, so what do you want with Lula Mae?
As if I didn't know.'

'Maybe I'm not ready for This-Is-It.'

'Well, if this *isn't* it you sure as hell better do something pretty soon because Lola's not someone you can fool
around with.'

'I'm not fooling around.'

'What else would you call it if you don't mean what you say?'

'I *do* mean what I say.'

'Wonderful, and the things you've said to Lola don't leave any room for side trips, do they.'

'Feelings aren't that simple,' says Max.

'Gee whiz!' says his mind. 'I never knew that. It's good that I have you to explain these things to me.'

'You and I,' says Max, 'don't seem to be getting along too well right now.'

'That's because I'm right and you're wrong. There are times when you know you'll be sorry for what you're going to do but you do it anyhow and then you're sorry.'

'William Blake said, "If the fool would persist in his folly he would become wise,"' says Max.

'Wise and all alone,' says his mind.

14

RESEARCH

February 1997. Lula Mae Flowers is a man-puller. That's what she does. She should really have that on her passport as her occupation: men are drawn to her as iron filings to a magnet. Max is somewhat off her beaten track but in the National Gallery she felt his eyes on her as she walked away and she's confident that he'll make contact soon.

The offices of Everest Technology are in Holborn, and two days after meeting Lula Mae, Max needs to research that part of town for a scene he might write in the novel for which he hasn't yet written Page One.

'I'm not going to ring her up,' he says to himself. 'I'll just stop by her office and probably she won't even be there. I'm leaving this entirely to chance.'

'What do you want,' says his mind, 'applause?'

Max enters the majestic glass tower of Everest Technology, goes to Reception, and says, 'Would you ring Lula Mae Flowers in Sales, please, and tell her that Max Lesser is here.'

'Is she expecting you?' says the receptionist.

'I think so,' says Max.

The receptionist rings up Lula Mae, then says to Max, 'Have a seat, she'll be right down.'

Max sinks into some expensive black leather and picks up a copy of *Fortune*. THE FUTURE IS NOW, says the cover as Lula Mae steps out of the lift and he feels a rush of blood to his head. He's read that the Sultan of Morocco once cited Virginia Mayo as tangible proof of the existence of God. Lula Mae is actually better looking than Virginia Mayo was.

'I had to do some research in this part of town,' says Max, 'so I thought I'd stop by and ask you to lunch.'

'I thought so too,' says Lula Mae, 'but I insist on taking you because you're my first writer.'

'That's surprising,' says Max, 'because there are a whole lot more of us than there are of you.'

Lula Mae flashes him a smile that makes him dizzy, takes his arm, and marches him off to The Garibaldi, her favourite lunchtime spot. There are lots of male pedestrians on the way, and when she passes, each one she passes says, 'Ah!'

The Garibaldi has a red signboard and a small statue of the hero of the Risorgimento in its window. '*Avanti, populo,*' says Max.

'Remember the Alamo,' says Lula Mae.

When they're seated and holding menus almost as big as the signboard, Lula Mae says, 'Do you like Chianti, Max? Say yes.'

'Yes,' says Max.

Lula Mae almost nods and a red-shirted waiter appears with a bottle, opens it, pours a taster, and offers it to Max. 'The lady will taste it,' says Max. Lula Mae gives him an approving look, tastes the wine, almost nods again, and the waiter pours. Lula Mae and Max raise their glasses to each other.

'"There never was a horse that couldn't be rode; there never was a cowboy that couldn't be throwed,"' says Lula Mae.

'"By the rivers of Babylon, there we sat down,"' says Max. Clink.

'So,' says Lula Mae, 'this girl you were with in the National Gallery, she's your girlfriend?'

'Yes,' says Max.

'But here you are,' says Lula Mae.

'I didn't know how not to be here,' says Max. 'You're a man-puller and you pulled me. If I'm too small you can throw me back.'

'Actually,' says Lula Mae, 'I like your non-Euclidean geometry.'

'I like yours too,' says Max.

'My flat is just a short walk from here,' says Lula Mae. 'A good place for research, quiet and out of the crush.'

'My kind of place,' says Max. By now they seem to have eaten something and finished the Chianti and off they go. Lula Mae's flat is tasteful and expensive. Among the books on her shelves Max sees George Eliot, Elizabeth Gaskell, Margaret Oliphant, Elmore Leonard, *Buddhist Wisdom Books*, Ortega y Gasset, H. P. Lovecraft, Robert Aickman, and Lafcadio Hearn.

'Jesus,' he says. 'You're a dark horse.'

'There's more to me than my going-away view, Cowboy,' says Lula Mae.

'When I was in high school,' says Max, 'girls like you only hung out with football heroes. If we'd been in the same school at the same time you wouldn't have looked at me.'

'Maybe not,' says Lula Mae, 'but I'm looking at you now.' There's music: Dusty Springfield singing, 'If you go away on this summer day, then you might as well take the sun away . . .' The song stops and is followed by some muted bossa nova. 'Grappa?' says Lula Mae.

'Yes, please,' says Max. 'How insensitive . . .' sings Astrud Gilberto, and is cut off short by Lula Mae.

'I like it better without music,' says Max.

'Me too,' says Lula Mae. She seems different now and Max is touched by the change. He kisses her gently, one thing leads to another, and here he is a little later, shaking his head on the Piccadilly Line.

Max's mind is silent for a while, riffling through the afternoon's action. Then it sings, 'But if you stay, I'll make you a day like no day has been or will be again . . .'

'What's this?' says Max.

'Just trying to remember the rest of that song,' says his mind. 'Are you wiser now, Cowboy?'

'Too soon to say,' says Max.

15

THE SCENT OF
LULA MAE FLOWERS

February 1997. Another Sunday, Hyde Park. Max and Lola at the Round Pond, watching the model boatmen and their model boats. 'Models are mysterious things,' says Lola.

'How so?' says Max. He enjoys the sight of the sail models tacking, the steam models chugging.

'Look at that Thames sailing barge,' says Lola. 'Totally realistic, and because it believes in itself there comes into being a model Thames running down to a model sea bounded by model continents on a whole model planet. Are you a model, Max?'

'What do you mean, Lola?'

'Is there a model Max-world extending outward from the realistic details of you?'

'Lola, I don't know what you're getting at.'

'No matter. Sometimes I talk crazy.' Her profile is needle-sharp in the lens of the chilly afternoon.

'Are you OK?' says Max.

'Do you mean, am I an OK person or are things OK with me?' She's looking past the boats and boatmen into the distance. The wind is blowing her hair in a way that goes to Max's heart.

'Are things OK with you?' he says.

'I don't know, Max. I can't help noticing that you're different today.'

'How am I different?'

'Do I smell Lula Mae on you?'

'You can't,' says Max. 'There's nothing to smell on me but me.' It's been a couple of days since he was with Lula Mae and he's had a shower this morning.

'I can smell her on your mind,' says Lola. 'It's something I wasn't expecting. I suppose I flattered myself that you'd have no interest left over for anyone else. When you came into the shop that December evening and said out loud that I was your destiny woman it was embarrassing but not dishonourable. It never occurred to me that you'd have a wandering eye.'

'Lola,' says Max, 'most men have a wandering eye. It's part of a genetic urge to spread one's seed as widely as possible. We're programmed that way.'

'Men are programmed to leave the toilet seat up too,' says Lola, 'but they can remember not to.'

Silence. Max and Lola both watching the model boats and noticing that the Round Pond has become as deep and wide as an ocean. The wind is raising little wavelets. The Thames barge, approaching a lee shore, comes about and bears away. The model boatmen are intent on their radio controls. Some of them have full-size wives and children with them. The sky grows darker, the afternoon is gathering in.

'It's getting colder,' says Lola. Max puts his arm around her but she doesn't press against him. She turns to look directly at him. Her eyes are unfathomable. Max waits for what she'll say next but she doesn't say anything.

16

DOING THEIR CHING

February 1997. Still that Sunday. Making their way out of the park through dusk and lamplight, Max and Lola are confronted by a very tall, very broad figure. 'Madam,' says the figure to Lola, 'is this man molesting you?'

'Basil!' says Lola.

'For it is indeed he,' says Basil, kissing Lola on both cheeks, mwah, mwah.

'Bit of a startler,' says Max.

'Joke, old man,' says Basil, extending a large right hand. 'Basil Meissen-Potts.'

'Ha ha,' says Max as his metacarpal bones splinter. 'Max Lesser.'

'Any relation to Solomon Lesser?'

'No. Who's he?'

'A pawnbroker who brought an action against Lady Glister a couple of years ago. She'd left a diamond necklace worth half a million with him at a time when she was a bit short of the readies. A year later when she redeemed it and had it reappraised for insurance she was told that the stones were paste. They'd been diamonds when she left the necklace with Lesser so she went back to have a word with him. In the

55

course of the conversation she beaned him with – what do you call those seven-branched candlesticks?'

'Candelabra?' says Max.

'Menorahs,' says Basil. 'She hit him with a brass menorah that was standing on the counter and fractured his skull. So he sued her and I had to defend her.'

'Who won?' says Max.

'We did. Lesser had to pay the full value of the diamonds plus what she'd given him to redeem the necklace plus court costs and damages for Lady Glister's post-traumatic stress.'

'You can't trust a Solomon,' says Max.

'Don't get me wrong,' says Basil. 'Some of my best friends are Solomons.'

'Thank you for sharing that with us,' says Lola to Basil. 'Where are you off to?'

'Claridge's. Bachelor party for Bill Twimbley-Sturt. Mwah, mwah. See you.' (This second mwah, mwah was unnecessary, thinks Max.) 'Nice meeting you, Max.'

'Same here,' says Max. 'I don't meet too many Meissen-Pottses.'

'We're an ethnic minority now,' says Basil. 'Take care.'

'Mind how you go,' says Max. As Basil recedes into the evening he says to Lola, 'I seem to remember your saying that he's a part of a kind of life you're accustomed to.'

'Have you got a copy of *The I Ching*?' says Lola.

'Sure. How come?'

'Because I want to do it. Let's go to your place.'

'OK,' says Max. 'I suppose we'll have to break the squalor barrier some time.' As they head for the Brompton Road, Lola pressing against his arm, Max has the feeling that she's afraid she'll be swept away by a wave of reality. Past Harrods, all picked out in lights like a vertical landing strip for low-flying shoppers, past Michelin House and the shops and lights in the Fulham Road as the shining rednesses of the 14 buses come and go, all the way home he feels around him the play of yes and no. When he opens his front door he notices how stale the air inside is. Now they're standing in his workroom which looks like something between a shipwreck and a bomb site. Bulging ranks of books look down from the shelves and totter in stacks on the floor along with dangerous heaps and sprawls of videotapes. Max's computer sits on a trestle table in a welter of paper and CDs. Discarded pages litter the floor under his chair.

'This works for you, does it?' says Lola.

'Oh yes. I don't know where everything is but I know where a lot of things are.' Max switches on lamps that contrive a pleasing balance of light and shadow on the clutter. He empties two armchairs, clears a little space on the floor, and gets *The I Ching* off the shelf. He opens a bottle of Jacob's Creek red and pours two glasses. 'Here's looking at you, Lola,' he says.

'Here's me looking right back,' says Lola. Clink.

Max takes three George V pennies from their pocket inside the back cover of the book. 'I haven't done this since I was thirty,' he says.

'Haven't you had any doubts since then?' says Lola.

'Lots,' says Max, 'but I don't seem to crave as much clarity as I used to.'

'This is going to be for both of us,' says Lola, 'so we'll each throw the coins three times.' She kneels on the floor, Max beside her. His throat aches with the poignancy of the lamplight on her cheek, on her hair. They throw the coins and get Hexagram 23, *Po/ Splitting Apart: above*, KEN – KEEPING STILL, MOUNTAIN, *below*, K'UN –

THE RECEPTIVE, EARTH, with six in the beginning
and six in second place. Lola and Max together skim the
opening lines of the text, then Max reads aloud THE
JUDGMENT:

> 'SPLITTING APART. It does not further one
> To go anywhere.'

'Great,' says Max. 'This book really knows how to hurt a
guy.'
'Here's THE IMAGE,' says Lola:

> 'The mountain rests on the earth:
> The image of SPLITTING APART.
> Thus those above ensure their position
> Only by giving generously to those below.'

'There you have it,' says Max. 'The only way to keep our
heads is to get busy with our lower parts.'
'I think you're right,' says Lola as she peels off her jumper.
'We can work out a fuller interpretation later.'

17

HOW IT WAS

February 1997. Still that Sunday. They'd grabbed each other as if to save themselves from drowning. Now that it's over they still cling, not wanting to let go. It's been a strange first time. Hexagram 23 was scary and unexpected in that it stated baldly what they both felt to be happening. Most of the time a hexagram is not to be taken literally: a judgment in which the superior man does this or that on a mountain is not necessarily about a man or a mountain. The thrower of the coins has a wide margin for interpretation. *The I Ching* doesn't tell you what's going to happen, it offers material that can show you how you feel about what's happening at the moment when you throw the coins. This physical act has in it your state of mind at that moment and evokes the book's response.

Still naked, Lola sits up with Max's arm around her. 'There were sixes in the beginning and in second place,' she says. 'That's two old yins changing Hexagram 23 to Hexagram 41.'

Max reaches for the book. '"*Sun/Decrease*,"' he reads: '"*above*, KEN – KEEPING STILL, MOUNTAIN; *below*, TUI – THE JOYOUS, LAKE."'

'Ah!' says Lola, THE JUDGMENT:

'Decrease combined with sincerity
Brings about supreme good fortune
Without blame.
One may be persevering in this.
It furthers one to undertake something.
How is this to be carried out?
One may use two small bowls for the sacrifice.'

'Our luck is changing for the better,' says Max.
'I like the text,' says Lola:

'Decrease does not under all circumstances mean something bad. Increase and decrease come in their own time.
What matters here is to understand the time and not to
try to cover up poverty with empty pretense.'

'And so on. Good, eh?'
'I promise to stop covering up my poverty,' says Max,
feeling irrationally that this line in the text might be a
comment on the size of his member.
'You know that's not what it means,' says Lola, following
his gaze. 'Here's THE IMAGE':

'At the foot of the mountain, the lake:
The image of DECREASE.
Thus the superior man controls his anger
And restrains his instincts.'

She reads on:

'The mountain stands as the symbol of a stubborn strength
that can harden into anger. The lake is the symbol of

unchecked gaiety that can develop into passionate drives at the expense of the life forces. Therefore decrease is necessary; anger must be decreased by keeping still, the instincts must be curbed by restriction. By this decrease of the lower powers of the psyche, the higher aspects of the soul are enriched.'

'I wish my soul had better higher aspects,' says Max.

'I do too,' says Lola, 'but I guess we'll have to make do with whatever aspects come to hand.'

'You're very gracious,' says Max. 'And for the rest of my life I'll remember how you looked at me when you took off your jumper.'

'I'm glad you appreciated that,' says Lola. 'I didn't take it off lightly. And bear in mind that we've now been warned about unchecked gaiety and passionate drives.'

'Right,' says Max. 'Will you stay here tonight?'

'OK,' says Lola. 'But first I'll have to check your gaiety.'

'I think you'll find it in good working order,' says Max.

18

THE WORST THAT
COULD HAPPEN

February 1997. 'All this with two women is going to end in tears,' says Max's mind.

'I know,' says Max. 'I'll have to sort myself out. I've been wondering, if I were writing about a guy in this situation, what would be the worst that could happen?'

'Well, he could lose his Lola, couldn't he. What could be worse than that?'

'Lola isn't with him every moment,' says Max. 'Much of her presence, her belovedness, is in his memory. And out of his memory comes his anticipation of the next time with her. If Lola leaves him he can still remember her. But if he loses his memory he loses her completely. So that's even worse. Maybe I could use that in a novel.'

'There might be some mileage in it,' says his mind.

'In Hindu mythology,' says Max, 'there's a dwarf demon of Forgetfulness called Apasmara Purusha. If this guy's Lola gets really pissed off she might find a way of putting Apasmara on to him to wipe out the memory of her.'

'That's really nasty,' says his mind. 'I like it. But what would get her that pissed off? Would sleeping with another woman one time do it?'

'I don't know,' says Max. 'It was just a passing thought. I doubt that I'll do anything with it – I'm not sure I like this guy well enough to write about him.'

19

A SHORT TIME WITH BASIL

February 1997. 'What is it with you and Max Lesser?' says Basil to Lola. They're having lunch at The Cheshire Cheese in Fleet Street. Lots of newspaper people there, upholding pints and their reputation for alcohol consumption while analysing the latest scandals, sports, and political news. Cheerful noises all around.

'Basil,' says Lola, 'I'll try to put this as gently as I can.'

'Put what?' says Basil.

'If,' says Lola, 'I were to ask my boyfriend to stand up, you'd have to remain seated.'

'It's like that, is it?'

'I'm afraid so.'

'This is a very sudden dismissal.'

'Not really. You and I have not been an item for quite a long time. What we had was more of a lifestyle thing than a romance.'

'And you're serious about Lesser, are you?'

'That's nothing you need concern yourself with.'

'I think it is. I'll always care about what happens to you.'

'That's sweet of you but try not to care too much.'

'Do you think you'll be happy with him?'

'Can we talk about something else? Have you had any interesting new cases?'

'I think this Jewish-intellectual fling of yours is a delayed adolescent revolt,' says Basil. 'This guy is no one for you to give your heart to. Let alone other parts. There'll come a time when you'll wish you still had good old suitable Baz.'

'When that happens,' says Lola, 'you'll be the second to know.'

'Have you read his books?' says Basil.

'I've read the most recent one.'

'*Any That You Can Not Put Downe* came out almost four years ago,' says Basil. 'He seems to be having a dry spell.'

'Three and a half years don't make a dry spell.'

'Have you read *Ten Thousand Several Doors* and *Turn Down An Empty Glass*?'

'No.'

'You should. They're long since out of print but I borrowed them from one of our clerks. Lesser always writes about the same thing: himself.'

'Lots of writers do that,' says Lola.

'But they don't all stick to a pattern the way Lesser does. In all three novels the protagonist betrays the woman who loves him and then she goes out of his life and he tries to win her back. In this last novel she's topped herself and put a curse on him and he's trying to get her ghost to lift the curse. I doubt that Ladbroke's would give very good odds on Lesser in the Fidelity Stakes.'

'You've really done your homework,' says Lola, 'but then you always do. It's nice to see you so excited about something. I'm sure that one of these days you'll find a woman who appreciates you.'

'I think you're going to be sorry about the choice you're making.'

'Maybe,' says Lola. 'But I won't be bored.'

20

GIRL TALK

February 1997. While Lola and Basil are at The Cheshire Cheese Lula Mae is at The Garibaldi .in High Holborn with Irma Lustig of Everest Technology Accounts. Like Lula Mae, Irma, originally from Stuttgart, is a head-turner of noble proportions. Herbert Wise, Personnel Manager at Everest, is known in the organisation as Herbie the Eye. He denies discrimination and claims that he rarely receives job applications from plain women.

'Who was that man I saw you with?' says Irma. 'Shorter than you.'

'The shorter ones try harder,' says Lula Mae. .

'He looked tired.'

'He doesn't spare himself.'

'Will you be seeing him again?'

'Probably. I've never had a man who didn't come back for more and it might be fun to be his muse for a while. He's a writer.'

'What's his name?'

'Max Lesser.'

'Never heard of him.'

'Neither had I but I don't think he's the kind of writer too many people hear of. There's a sadness about him that appeals to me. When I met him he was with this upper-class girl who seemed a little too sure of herself.'

'So you're going to make her less sure?'

'Maybe.'

'Any future in this for you?'

'I'm not thinking futures at the moment. He's interesting and I'm interested. He's more appreciative than the kind of men I'm used to and I like that.'

'You should invest your time more wisely,' says Irma. 'One day men will stop sighing when you pass.'

'That won't be for a while yet,' says Lula Mae.

Irma lowers her eyes to her empty glass for a fraction of a second and a red-shirted waiter instantly appears with two more grappas. '*Prosit*,' she says.

'Likewise,' says Lula Mae. 'So how are things with you?'

'I'm building a careful portfolio, very conservative,' says Irma, 'and I'm acquiring the odd property. I expect to be financially independent by the time I'm thirty-five.'

'What about affairs of the heart?'

'I get one or two offers every week to be somebody's trophy wife and there are always plenty of men who want to get into my knickers but that isn't where my heart is. The kind of men I might like to meet are usually afraid to approach me. I envy you your interesting Max, even if it comes to nothing.'

'It's a funny thing,' says Lula Mae. 'He's not really my type but for years he's been craving recognition from my kind of woman.'

'What happens if you stop giving it to him?'

'Who knows what the future holds?'

'Just be careful, Lula Mae.'

'Sometimes I get tired of being careful,' says Lula Mae.

2 I

MOE LEVY'S BURDEN

March 1997. Here's Max at his desk. Except for the odd
engagement or research [sic] trip, this is where he puts in
ten hours a day, seven days a week. All those hours and
no Page One? Life is hard but today Max has the feeling
that there's going to be a breakthrough. The wallpaper on
his Fujitsu/Siemens screen is Winslow Homer's *The Gulf
Stream*. In it a black man leans on his elbow on the slanting
deck of his dismasted and rudderless boat while sharks circle
him. Maybe there's been a hurricane. The sea is wild and
there's a waterspout in the distance. The boat can't be much
more than twenty feet. No visible damage to the hull. Will
he make it? Sometimes Max thinks yes, sometimes no. Today
he's thinking yes.

'OK,' he says to the computer, 'let's do it. Going for Page
One.' Fujitsu/Siemens has heard this before but it puts up
a blank page for Max as if it takes him seriously. Max has
been giving this some thought and already he's got a name
for his protagonist: Morris Levy. 'We'll call him Moe,' he
says. MOE LEVY'S BURDEN will be the first chapter if
Max gets lucky. Having typed that heading he sighs and sits
back, hoping that nothing bad is looking over his shoulder.

He's in his normal working panic. This is still 1997 and there's nothing threatening him except the blank page. He's afraid of what might appear on it as he types.

He gets Moe out of bed and out of the house. So far, so good. Moe's going to meet his friend Fergal Hagerty for lunch at Il Fornello, so he takes the District Line to Earls Court, then changes to the Piccadilly for Russell Square. Coming out of the tube station Moe makes his way past the newsagent and the luggage stall. His head feels strange and for a moment the world stops being there. Then it comes back with a little jolt and he's aware of a terrible stench. It's like the smell of a backed-up toilet in an empty house with broken windows. Out of the corner of his eye Moe sees something following him. Is it a dog? A cat? It's a little man, black as ebony, long body, very short arms and legs, large head, big ugly baby-face. He's inching along on his belly and writhing like a dog that's been run over. Moe looks around. Lots of foot traffic but nobody is stepping on the dwarf. Nobody is taking any notice at all. The smell is almost making Moe throw up but he wants to do the decent thing. He says to the dwarf, 'Are you all right?'

'Closer,' says the dwarf. His voice is like dead leaves skittering on the floor of that empty house with the backed-up toilet.

'Not sure this is a good idea,' says Moe's mind.

Moe comes closer. Like a jumping spider the dwarf springs off the pavement and there he is in Moe's arms. 'Hold me,' he says, sobbing a little. This is a very heavy dwarf and Moe tries to put him down but his arms and hands have lost the ability to let go.

'Shit,' says Max, as he reads what he's typed. 'Where's

this coming from?' He remembers thinking about using Apasmara Purusha but what he's written is a little too real, like something that's already happened. Or is going to.

On the Fujitsu/Siemens screen the cursor is beating like a heart at the place where the next line should start. Nothing happens. Behind the cursor Moe gets tired of waiting in the dark. 'What now?' he says to Max. 'I'm standing here holding this heavy stinking dwarf and I'm waiting for my next thing to do.'

'You're stuck there,' says Max. 'All of a sudden your memory is gone. Apasmara made you forget everything.'

'Why?'

'He was sent to do that.'

'Who sent him?'

'A woman you can't remember. She sent Apasmara to take away all memory of her.'

'Why? What would make her do that?'

'What you did.'

'What did I do?'

'I don't know.'

'What came before what I did?'

'You loved each other.'

'OK, we loved each other. What then?'

'I don't know.'

'Think! Explore your material. What did I do?'

'I'm telling you, I don't know.'

'That's great. You've got me holding this lousy dwarf and you don't know why and you don't know what's coming next.'

'Moe, I'm sorry to leave you holding the dwarf, I really am.'

'You could delete that part and back up to where we were

71

before he jumped into my arms. Come on, you can at least do that much for me.'

'I'm sorry, Moe, that might stop the next thing from coming to me and I daren't risk it. Besides, Apasmara's not real, he's only a hallucination. The weight and the smell are all in your mind.'

'Wonderful. Thanks a lot. I'll see you around.'

Max quits the word processor programme and goes back to the Winslow Homer painting that is his screen wallpaper. But instead of that boat in the Gulf Stream he sees Noah's Ark stranded on the mountains of Ararat. The raven flies out, loops the loop once and *The Gulf Stream* returns. 'Sorry,' says Max's mind.

'No problem,' says Max.

22

FURTHER RESEARCH

March 1997. Lula Mae with no clothes on is a feast for the eye and two or three other senses. Max is grazing quietly on her when she says, 'Max?'

'What, Lula Mae?'

'How come you're here with me?'

'What a question!'

'I don't want the obvious answer – most men like a bit of strange and most men who see me want to have me. I'm looking for the you/me specifics that resulted in our sleeping together for what is now the fifth time. Don't you wonder where it's coming from and where it's going?'

'When I'm with you I'm not thinking of that,' says Max.

'What about when you're not with me?'

'Then I try not to think of it.'

'Say more.'

'Much of the time I don't understand what I do. And all of the time I don't understand my life. Do you understand yours?'

'Until now I don't think I've tried to. What about you and Lola?'

'What do you want to know?'

'Are you in love with her?'

'Yes.'

'And is she in love with you?'

'Looks that way.'

'You're not sure?'

'She's very careful with words.'

'But you've slept with her, yes?'

'I feel disloyal, talking about her like this.'

'That's a hot one: you don't feel disloyal shagging me but you don't like to talk about her while you're in my bed.'

'Life is full of anomalies, Lula Mae.'

'You haven't answered my question.'

'OK, I've slept with her.'

At this point Max's mind is unable to refrain from a little cluck of disapproval.

'What?' says Max.

'You know very well what,' says his mind. 'Shtupping Lula Mae is already an intrusion into Lola's privacy but this kind of talk makes it worse.'

'Lola's privacy!'

'That's right. Your nakedness and your lovemaking are private to Lola. Now you've exposed Lola's nakedness to Lula Mae.' Another little cluck.

'I'm not a good man,' says Max.

'Could do better,' says his mind.

'Hello?' says Lula Mae. 'Are you there?'

'More or less,' says Max.

'If you and Lola are in love,' says Lula Mae, 'why did you look me up in Holborn?'

'You told me where you worked and then you gave me your going-away view. I'd have had to be dead not to respond.'

'OK, that was one time. What about since then? What are you looking for with me?'

'I don't know. I guess I'm just greedy. What about you? Your attractions aren't just physical, you could pretty well have any man you fancied. Why are you spending time with me?'

'When it started I was a little bit trying to make up for all the girls you couldn't get in high school. Your face is full of never-had-enough and I was touched by it.'

'And the greatest of these is charity,' says Max. 'You're a real Christian, Lula Mae.'

'In my way. But now it's become something else.'

'What?'

'I haven't figured it out yet, but it's got me taking a long hard look at myself.'

'And what are you seeing?'

'A woman who's been walking through a maze where all the pathways bring you out again and you never reach the centre.'

'What's at the centre?'

'Maybe I'll never know. In the meantime . . .' She rolls over on to Max and he stops asking questions.

23

FREYING NOW?

March 1997. Ring, ring. With the smell of Lula Mae still in his nostrils and the taste of her in his mouth Max picks up the phone and says hello.

'Hi,' says Lola. 'It's me.'

'Hi,' says Max. That voice of hers! Always that clear stream in a dappled wood.

'I'm taking a day off,' says Lola. 'This Friday is the vernal equinox.'

'Yes,' says Max, 'the same thing happened last year.'

'And Friday, of course, is Freya's day,' says Lola, 'very auspicious for what I have in mind.'

'What's that?'

'It's a mystery drive to a picnic at a special place. Can I pick you up around ten?'

'I'll be ready.' After they ring off he says to himself, 'This isn't right, I must wind things up with Lula Mae.'

'And not before time,' says his mind.

'I know,' says Max. 'At first I thought she was someone I could walk away from and no harm done on either side but it's not that simple.'

'Surprise, surprise.'

'It's a funny thing,' says Max, 'she could have any man she wanted. But I have the feeling that she's always wanted a kind of man she's never had.'

'And you're it?'

'Well, yes. I'm nothing much to look at and I'm not a great lover but it might be that I appreciate her in a way no other man has.'

'I'd have to have a heart of stone not to fall about laughing at that,' says his mind.

'You may scoff.'

'I just did.'

'I'll see her one last time,' says Max, 'and I'll tell her it's over.'

'That's the way to do it,' says his mind.

24

GIRL TALK 2

March 1997. The moon waxes and wanes, the sea responds with spring tides and neap tides, the waves fling up the pebbles with a grating roar and draw back again as they did when Matthew Arnold listened on Dover Beach.

A few days after Max and Lula Mae's fifth get-together Lula Mae and Irma Lustig are lunching again at The Garibaldi. Irma flickers an eyelid and a red-shirted waiter appears with a bottle of Chianti. He opens it, pours a taster for Irma, she tastes it and fractionally inclines her head. The waiter pours two glasses and vanishes. '*Zum wohl*,' says Irma.

'Happy days,' says Lula Mae.

'What's new?' says Irma.

'I'm pregnant,' says Lula Mae.

'I'll drink to that,' says Irma.

'I thought you told me to be careful.'

'And you carefully got pregnant. You're not going to tell me it was an accident?'

'Not really. All of a sudden I didn't feel like taking the pill.'

'Ovulation makes one hot to trot.'

'Yup.'

'Your interesting Max was the lucky man?'

'Lucky or not, he's the one.'

'I seem to remember that he craved recognition from your kind of woman. Do you think he craved this much?'

'I doubt it.'

'Are you keeping it?'

'Yes.'

'Have you told him?'

'No.'

'Are you going to tell him?'

'I haven't decided.'

'Why not?'

'He says he's in love with Lola Bessington.'

'Miss Too–Sure–of–Herself?'

'Yes. I'd feel bad about coming between them but I doubt that she's the right woman for him. He needs someone whose moral standards aren't too exacting.'

'And you are the right woman?'

'I have doubts about that too. Sometimes I think being a single mother is more my style but at other times the idea of a proper family is tempting.'

'Everest Technology gets more and more complicated,' says Irma, 'but there's nothing as complicated as men and women.'

'And we all come without manuals,' says Lula Mae.

While Lula Mae and Irma tuck into their lasagne and drink their Chianti the not-yet-risen moon is waxing, comet Hale-Bopp trails its fiery tail unseen, night and day are approaching parity, and Lola Bessington, between customers at the Coliseum Shop, listens to *Die Winterreise* with tears running down her cheeks.

79

25

BOY TALK

March 1997. The vernal equinox will be on Friday. This is Thursday. Lula Mae will be seeing a client in the New King's Road and Max has arranged to meet her at The White Horse in Parson's Green at half-past five. He's pretty sure he's going to tell her it's over but he's not altogether sure it is. He's having lunch now at Coffee Republic in Fulham Broadway. He's grateful for the little hubbub of noise and people around him, he'd rather not be alone with his mind. He's finished his sandwich, and while he lingers over his second coffee the lunchtime rush has subsided and he notices, alone at a table across the room, a short white-haired man who could pass for an older version of himself. He recognises Harold Klein, the art historian, from his TV series, *The Innocent Eye*. Klein seems approachable so Max approaches. 'Mr Klein,' he says, 'may I join you?'

'Please do,' says Klein. 'I know you from your photo. I've read your books and liked them. They're the kind of thing I might have written if I could write novels.'

'Thank you,' says Max, 'I'm flattered. I enjoyed *The Innocent Eye* but what really knocked me out was your monograph on Odilon Redon.'

'Well, he tells it like it is,' says Klein, 'and I tried to do the same.'

'You succeeded brilliantly.'

'You're very kind,' says Klein.

'I feel that I can talk to you,' says Max.

'So do I,' says Klein. 'So talk.'

'I'm too sober,' says Max. 'Let's go get pissed.'

'OK,' says Klein, and they remove to The Pickled Pelican in Moore Park Road. Max brings pints of Pedigree, doubles of Glenfiddich, and bags of crisps to their table. 'Mud in your eye,' he says as they clink glasses.

'Down the hatch,' says Klein as the football on the TV bursts into a roar. 'Unburden yourself.'

'What did you say?' shouts Max.

'Unburden yourself,' shouts Klein.

'I'm not a good man,' shouts Max as the TV goes quiet and the rest of the pub turns to look at him.

'That makes two of us,' says Klein.

Max then spills his guts and tells Klein all about Lola and Lula Mae, his doubts, his fears, his indecision and his confusion. Klein listens patiently and nods his head while Max keeps the Pedigree and Glenfiddich coming. When Max has finished, they down their third boilermakers in silence. At length Klein, with a Godfather gesture, index finger pointing upward, says, 'I look at you and I see myself twenty-five years ago, always greedy for more love and other love. Always unfaithful.'

'What can you tell me?' says Max.

'Probably,' says Klein, 'you're a little bit in love with Lula Mae and maybe she's a little bit in love with you. If she weren't, she'd have moved on by now. You want to end it with her and at the same time you don't. You don't want to end it with Lola but you're backing away from This-Is-It. Shall I be honest with you?'

'Not necessarily,' says Max.

'You're bad news,' says Klein. 'If you care about these women at all, the best thing you can do is get out of their lives before you get in any deeper. Better a small heartbreak now than a big one later.' With that, Klein falls asleep. Max wakes him up, they visit the Gents, then leave The Pickled Pelican.

26

TWO LITTLE WORDS

March 1997. Max at The White Horse. The day is cold and windy but he doesn't want to sit inside. The smoke and the uproar of the braying crowd make him feel trapped. He gets a pint of Bass at the bar and takes it to an outside table. There he sits looking past the Parson's Green Clinic and Lady Margaret's School towards the corner of the New King's Road where Lula Mae will appear.

'Better a small heartbreak now,' says his mind.

'When she comes around that corner,' says Max, 'my heart will leap up at the sight of her. Then I'll tell her it's all over.'

'Are you in love with her?' says his mind.

'I'm so comfortable with her!' says Max. 'I don't know if it's love but we really like each other.'

There she is now, coming around the distant corner. Max's heart leaps up and so does the rest of him. He waves to Lula Mae and she waves back as she walks towards him.

'Ah!' sighs a nearby drinker.

Max's eyes fill with Lula Mae. He tries to imagine her as a little girl with pigtails, sitting on her father's lap while he reads her Lovecraft's *The Call of Cthulhu*. His throat aches.

'Hi, Cowboy,' she says.

'Hi,' says Max. Big hug, big kiss. 'What'll you have?'

'Same as you,' says Lula Mae. When Max returns from the bar they lift their glasses to each other.

'Here's how,' says Max.

'I think we already know how,' says Lula Mae. 'I'm pregnant.'

Max notices an aeroplane high overhead. Is it trailing a banner that says THIS IS IT? He looks back at Lula Mae. 'I'll drink to that,' he says. '*L'haim!* To life!'

'*L'haim*,' says Lula Mae. 'You think I should have it?'

'Of course you should have it,' he says. 'A child from you and me! Wow.'

'You're not going to ask me if I'm sure you're the father?'

'If I weren't, you'd have told me,' says Max.

'You just got a foot taller,' says Lula Mae.

'There's more to me than Lesser,' says Max. Big hug, big kiss, broad grins, more schmoozing, two more pints. 'So what's our next move?' he says.

'What do you mean?' says Lula Mae.

'Well, some people when they have a child, they all live together and it's a family,' says Max. 'Sometimes the parents get married.'

'Are you proposing to me?'

'I've been listening to the words coming out of my mouth,' says Max, 'and I don't really know what I'm doing.'

'Take deep breaths and calm down. It's not as if my father's coming after you with a shotgun.'

'I know that,' says Max, 'and I'm calm. What do you think we should do?'

'Double scotches,' says Lula Mae. 'My shout. This requires careful thought.'

27

URSA MAJOR, LESSER MINOR

21 March 1997. Morning of the vernal equinox. Max is waiting on his front steps with a sleeping bag and a small rucksack. At ten o'clock Lola pulls up in a seriously green E-type convertible with a black top. 'Hi,' she says.

'Hi,' says Max. 'Nice ride.'

'Birthday present from Daddy. It's a '62, three point eight litre. They made them with bigger engines later but Daddy says this one's a Stradivarius and it does a ton without breathing hard.'

'I'm breathing hard just looking at it,' says Max.

'This colour is British Racing Green,' says Lola.

'A fast colour,' says Max.

'Nothing illegal today,' says Lola. She notes the sleeping bag and smiles. 'Expecting to get lucky?'

'You never know,' says Max.

'Put it in the boot with mine,' says Lola. The picnic hamper takes up most of the boot but Max jams his things in and sinks into the leather upholstery beside Lola. They kiss good morning, the Jaguar roars and they're off. Up the North End Road, through West Kensington, on to the Great West Road, Hogarth Roundabout, and the M4. Motorway miles moving towards them, passing under them, the Jaguar purring sweetly at seventy and sometimes more. 'When *is* your birthday?' says Max.

'Today,' says Lola. 'I'm a vernal–equinoctial kind of girl. My first quarter–century.'

'You never told me,' says Max. 'I'd have got you a present.'

'You're my present,' says Lola. She kisses her fingers and touches them on his lips.

'We're heading west,' says Max. 'Where to?'

Lola smiles and says, 'You'll see.' The Jaguar swallows the miles as the names of towns grow large in front of them, small behind them. Exits beckon here and there with forceful arrows. Max and his mind are working on what he'll say to Lola. O God, she's so beautiful, so aristocratic, so deep, so wild at heart, so everything he longed for just a short time ago. Longs for still but . . .

'Lola,' says his mind as he rehearses possible openings, 'I don't know how to say this but I guess the simplest way is the best. Lula Mae is pregnant and I'm the father.'

'You're very quiet,' says Lola.

'I fall into a travel trance sometimes,' says Max.

'Me too,' says Lola, 'except when I'm driving.' She's humming that Dusty Springfield song. 'But if you stay,' says her humming, 'I'll make you a day like no day that's been or ever will be . . .'

'Lola,' says Max's mind, 'the days and nights I've had with you have been like no other days and nights I've ever known . . .'

'Sickening,' says Max. 'Brutal was better.'

' . . . the pebbles according to size,' says Lola.

'What?' says Max.

'Chesil Beach,' says Lola. 'Ever been there?'

'No. I've read about it though – it's a shingle storm beach where the waves sort the pebbles according to size.'

'That's what I just said,' says Lola. 'It's not far from Dorchester. Did you know about Veästa?'

'No.'

'Chesil Beach sea monster, last seen in 1995.'

'There'll always be monsters,' says Max. 'God made them along with Virginia Mayo and . . . Chesil Beach.' He was going to say Lula Mae Flowers but stopped in time.

'Events,' says Max's mind, 'sort people according to size. It seems I'm one of the smaller ones.'

'What events are you talking about?' says Lola.

'Was I speaking out loud?' says Max.

'Unless I'm hearing voices,' says Lola. 'I say again, what events?'

'Just reviewing my life,' says Max, 'as a drowning man might do.'

'Max, are you drowning?'

'I'm fine,' says Max.

'How's the writing going?' says Lola.

'On the novel front,' says Max, 'I may or may not have a protagonist but so far no Page One. On the children's side there's Charlotte Prickles waiting for a new story which I haven't got. That's two No Page Ones.'

Lola puts a sympathetic hand on Max's thigh. 'That's happened before though, hasn't it?'

'Many, many times,' says Max.

'And you always work through it and you manage to live pretty well off your writing,' says Lola.

'Thanks to Charlotte,' says Max. Sudden vision of her lying flattened in the road. No, no, please.

'Those books still bring in royalties!' says Lola.

'Oh yes, I've done seven and they're all alive and well. That's how I can afford to write novels. This is the first time you've asked me about my finances.'

'Well, you know, one day I might want to introduce you to my parents and I've got to be prepared.'

'I've seen photographs of your father in *The Times*,' says Max. 'He looks like the last days of the Raj.'

'Somewhat to the right of that, actually,' says Lola.

'And I've seen photos of your mother in *Tatler*, so I know where you got your looks.'

'The fruit doesn't fall far from the tree,' says Lola.

'Speaking of fruit, I could use an apple or a banana right now,' says Max.

'No snacks,' says Lola. 'We don't get to have the picnic until we're on top of where we're going.'

'Maiden Castle?' says Max.

'Right,' says Lola. 'Have you been there?'

'Not yet,' says Max. 'It's one of those things I've seen in dreams but not in real life.'

'What kind of dreams?'

'All I remember is wideness and greenness and the wind.'

'By day or by night?'

'Always by day, in the golden light of late afternoon.'

'Never in the morning?'

'Not that I remember.'

PUDDLETOWN, says a sign. An arrow points to WEYMOUTH and Lola turns as directed. At Maumbury Rings she gets on to the road that takes them to MAIDEN CASTLE. 'Mai Dun is the old name,' she says as they pull into the car park. And here it is. Not looming very high but very wide, happed in ancient grasses green and brown and tawny. Sheep graze on the layered years. The wind sighs, the ghosts also. Max and his mind as well. The day is bright and sunny but on the cool side with a fresh breeze blowing.

Although this is the beginning of the weekend there aren't too many cars in the car park. There are information boards and Max wants to read them but Lola pulls him away. 'Facts will just get between you and it,' she says. 'Mai Dun is beyond facts.'

Carrying hamper, sleeping bags and blanket, Max and Lola start up the brown path to the access track. 'Why is this day different from other days?' says Max's mind.

'You know why,' says Max.

'You could have called off this trip after you saw Lula Mae,' says his mind.

'I didn't know how,' says Max.

'This day is different from other days,' says Lola.

'I know,' says Max. There are little white daisies and small yellow flowers by the track. 'What do you call this yellow one?' says Max.

'Primula,' says Lola.

They climb to the inner rampart and feel the sky around them. Looking south past the outer ramparts and ditches they take in the tree-lined fields and meadows undulating in easy sweeps to the blue distance. 'This is the place,' says Lola.

'That's what Brigham Young said,' says Max's mind. 'Women were no problem for him.'

'I don't believe that,' says Max. 'Be quiet.'

They spread their blanket and open the hamper which is full of good things including three bottles of Cristal in icy sleeves. At a nod from Lola, Max uncorks the first bottle and Lola takes it from him and pours a little on the ground. 'Absent friends,' she says.

'They're probably used to something a little less expensive,' says Max. He pours two glasses and he and Lola drink to each other.

Lola takes the ribbon from her hair, ties it to a long stem of grass where it flutters like a tiny banner. 'They're all around us,' she says, 'the ones who lived here on Mai Dun thousands of years ago. The wind that's blowing my ribbon blew the smoke of their fires. Nothing goes away. I chose this day to come here because it's the vernal equinox, the first day of spring when the night and the day are the same length.'

'The light and the dark equal,' says Max as his mind gives him that image: light on the left, dark on the right.

The hamper now gives up its contents: melon and prosciutto, ciabatta and roast peppers, pâté and salami, ripe Camembert and oat crackers. Max uncorks the second bottle which goes down even more smoothly than the first. The third follows in due course.

There are only a few other people, some with dogs, all with cameras taking pictures of the ramparts and ditches, the views and one another. Lola and Max take out their cameras and photograph each other and their picnic spread. 'I want to stay here till midnight,' says Lola. She and Max press close to each other as the afternoon grows colder. Evening comes and they're alone with the sky all around them. They zip the sleeping bags together, take off their clothes, get inside and make each other warm. Max's rucksack provides a bottle of Courvoisier which dissolves any vestigial chill. Evening becomes night and they lie listening to the speaking of the earth and the wind in the grasses of Mai Dun. Noah's Ark appears, stranded in Max's mind from his father's memory of long ago. The raven flies out, loops the loop once, and is gone. 'What does this mean?' Max asks his mind.

'I can only tell you what I know,' says his mind, 'and I don't know what this image means or why it haunts us.'

The almost-full moon rises and looks down on the banks and ditches of the hill-fort, the labial configurations at either end meant to baffle invaders or possibly honour the white goddess. Despite the paling of the sky the stars are clearly visible, brighter than in London. Burning and flickering, they send their light from before the age of dinosaurs, the Babylonian exile, the fall of Rome, the sack of Jerusalem. 'See the Great Bear?' says Lola. 'Ursa Major?'

'The Big Dipper,' says Max, 'and the North Star.'

'Polaris,' says Lola. Gripping Max's hand, she murmurs rapidly, 'Alkaid, Mizar, Alioth, Megrez, Phecda, Merak, Dubhe.'

'What was that?' says Max.

'The names of the seven stars of Ursa Major. Say them after me: Alkaid.'

'Alkaid.'

'Mizar.'

'Mizar.'

'Alioth.'

'Alioth.'

'Megrez.'

'Megrez.'

'Phecda.'

'Phecda.'

'Merak.'

'Merak.'

'Dubhe.'

'Dubhe.'

'Max and Lola,' says Lola.

'Stop,' says Max's mind. 'This is a serious ritual. What are you doing?'

'Lola and Max,' says Max. He thinks he might faint.

'That's it then,' says Lola. 'That's us with the seven and the absent friends. And Hale-Bopp says yes.'

'Who's Hale-Bopp?'

'The comet. It's up there in the northwest between Andromeda and Cassiopeia. Very bright, although you can see the tail better on moonless nights.' She takes Max's head in her hands and aims him at the comet. 'See it?'

'Got it. You seem to be good friends with the stars.'

'Yes,' says Lola, 'good friends with the stars. I'm pregnant.'

When Eve first said those two words to Adam she watched his face closely. Lola's doing the same with Max.

'Wow,' says Max.

'Say more,' says Lola.

'Speechless,' says Max. Big hug, big kiss.

'So you're happy about it?' says Lola.

'Like crazy,' says Max.

28

OVERLOAD

March 1997. It's 01:15 so it's the 22nd now. Lola has just made her announcement and Max has said his very few words. It'll take about ten minutes to come down from Mai Dun and walk back to the car. Not much traffic at this time in the morning so it's maybe two and a half hours back to Fulham. Say a total of two hours and forty minutes that have to be filled with something. 'What am I going to say?' Max says to his mind. 'What am I going to do?'

'Don't ask me,' says his mind. 'What we have here is overload. All I want to do is be somewhere else.'

'That makes two of us,' says Max.

'Two of us what?' says Lola.

'Two of us with something to think about.'

'You said you're happy about it but you don't seem happy,' she says.

'It's a lot to take in,' says Max. He squeezes her hand but she doesn't squeeze back.

'I've never come here with anyone else,' says Lola. 'Never said the names of the seven at midnight on this day of the year with anyone before.'

'I'll never forget this day and night as long as I live,' says Max.

'You look, you sound, as if you're saying goodbye,' says Lola.

'The present is always saying goodbye to the past,' says Max.

'You never used to talk bollocks like that,' says Lola. 'Wait a minute – do I smell Lula Mae Flowers again?'

'Deny everything,' says Max's mind.

'I cheat,' says Max, 'but I don't lie.' Saying it out loud. Did he mean to?

'So you've slept with her,' says Lola.

'I'm afraid so,' says Max.

'Stop there,' says his mind, 'or you'll be doing more harm than you can ever undo.'

'Say more,' says Lola. 'I need to know the whole thing so this day can be complete.'

'She's . . .' Max pauses as he looks into the abyss.

'O my God,' says Lola. 'Don't say it. Say it.'

'Pregnant,' says Max.

'Pregnant!' says Lola. She recoils as if she's been smacked in the face with a dead mackerel. 'You bastard! And while your baby's growing in her belly you crawl on top of me and do me one more time for good measure. You're disgusting. Stupid, stupid me! I brought you here and we did our stupid little ritual because I thought I was your one and only and you were mine. I thought I was your destiny woman – that's what you called me in the Coliseum Shop and everyone turned to look, remember?'

'I remember.'

'And this would be our destiny child,' says Lola.

'We need to talk about all of this,' says Max feebly.

'No, we don't.' They're in the car now, the Jaguar snarls, leaps forward with a VROOM, and they're off to the Weymouth Road and up to the A35.

Max can't think of anything useful to say and Lola preserves a stony silence as she looks straight ahead into the darkness and the yellow motorway lights. Names and numbers of exits grow large in front of them, small behind them. Arrows point to right and left, up and down. 'You're driving too fast,' says Max. 'Remember, we've had quite a bit to drink.'

'Yes,' says Lola.

'Where did the raven go?' thinks Max as the car veers off the motorway, plunges down an embankment, and crashes into something concrete with numbers on it.

29

THE MOUNTAINS OF ARARAT

April 1997. Afternoon. 'What about the raven?' says Max.

'All I know,' says his mind, 'is that Noah sent it forth and "it went to and fro until the waters were dried up from off the earth".'

'What then?' says Max. 'I want to know more.'

'That's all it says in Genesis, just what I told you.'

'Maybe,' says Max, 'that raven is still out there, looping the loop, doing aerobatics, flying up a storm.'

'Well, they *are* great flyers,' says his mind. 'This one must have gone crazy, cooped up in the Ark for almost a year. So I expect it would loop the loop and so on when it got out of there.'

'What about Mrs Raven? There were two of everything but this bird took off on his own and was never heard from again. Mid-flood crisis? What?'

'Don't know,' says Max's mind.

'The mountains of Ararat,' says Max, 'are they behind the boiler?'

'Yes.'

'But the raven's not behind the boiler.'

'Nevermore,' says Max's mind.

'Hello,' says a nurse. 'Welcome back.'

'It's great to be back,' says Max. 'Where?'

'Poole Hospital,' says the nurse. 'How're you feeling?'

'Not sure,' says Max. 'When is this?'

'Sixth of April,' says the nurse.

'When did I get here?' says Max.

'Twenty-second of March.'

'Not today.'

'Right.'

'What?' says Max.

'You've been in a coma and you've just come out of it.'

'Lola?'

'Lyla,' says the nurse.

'What Lyla?' says Max.

'Me Lyla,' says the nurse. 'I thought you were speaking my name.' She shows him her name badge: LYLA MURPHY.

'I wanted to ask about my girlfriend, Lola Bessington,' says Max. 'She was driving the Ark. Cark. Car.'

'No injuries other than minor cuts and bruises and she was a bit shaken up,' says Lyla. 'She tested over the limit and had a summons to answer. She was discharged a couple of days after she was admitted. Her parents came and picked her up.'

'She's pregnant. Is the baby all right?'

'I don't know anything about that.'

'Could you try to find out for me, please?'

'OK.'

'When can I go home?'

'Probably in a day or two. They might want to do a follow-up EEG but I doubt it. I'll see if I can find out about the other. Stay quiet for a while, OK?'

'OK. Thanks, Lula Mae.'

'Lyla, me.'

'Sorry. Names move around behind the boiler.'

'What boiler is that?'

'The big black lying-down one.'

'With names behind it?'

'Alkaid, Mizar, Alioth, Megrez, Phecda, Merak, Dubhe.'

'I was thinking of going to Dubai,' says Lyla. 'Nurses make good money there.'

Later she reports that there was nothing about pregnancy in Lola's admission report. Max takes this to mean that she's been told not to tell him anything.

That afternoon he's moved out of Intensive Care to a ward with three other men, all of them old. One of them keeps wetting the bed. His name is Byron. Another stares at Max and moves his mouth but no words come out. He's Neville. The third is Fred. He was in the submarine service in World War II. 'Were you ever hit by depth charges?' says Max. 'Wouldn't be here if we'd ever taken a direct hit,' says Fred. 'Close ones sometimes, the plates would start to buckle and you'd get some water coming in but you've got to expect that sort of thing from time to time.'

A nurse called Laura takes Max's temperature, blood pressure and pulse. She gets an oxygen reading from a thing clipped to his finger. 'How am I?' says Max.

'Blood pressure's a little low,' says Laura, and writes up his chart.

'You've got to expect that sort of thing from time to time,' says Max. Lying on the bottom and maintaining silence, he waits for the depth charges, feels the shock of the explosions, sees the water spurting in as the plates buckle.

30

PHONE TALK

'Seven three eight five, seven two seven seven,' says a male voice, very refined.

'I'm calling Lola Bessington,' says Max. 'Have I got the right number?'

'Miss Bessington's calls are being diverted to this number,' says the voice.

'Whom am I speaking to, please?' says Max.

'This is Poole,' says Poole.

'Poole is where I'm calling from. This is Max Lesser.'

'Yes, Mr Lesser. Was there anything else?'

'Can you tell me how she is?'

'No,' says Poole. 'I am not able to do that. Goodbye.'

'Chambers,' says a crisp female voice answering Max's next call.

'I'd like to speak to Basil Meissen-Potts, please,' says Max.

'Who's calling, please?' says Ms Crisp.

'Max Lesser.'

'Mr Meissen-Potts is out of the country at present.'

'When do you expect him back?'

'Try again in two weeks.'

'Thank you,' says Max, and rings Poole again.

'Seven three eight five, seven two seven seven,' says Poole.

'Max Lesser again,' says Max. 'Can I speak to Lady Bessington?'

'Lady Bessington cannot be reached at this time,' says Poole.

'Lord Bessington, then?'

'I'll have to put you on hold for a moment,' says Poole. Silence. No music.

The next voice has a Victorian moustache and wears a sola topi. 'Bessington here,' it says, switching a riding crop against its boot.

'Lord Bessington,' says Max, 'this is Max Lesser. I was hoping to talk to Lola.'

'Yes, no doubt you were.'

'Can you at least tell me how she is?'

'I'm a rather busy man,' says Lord Bessington, 'but if you'd like to speak to my secretary I'll try to squeeze you in for a horsewhipping.'

'Would that make you feel better?' says Max.

'Yes, it would give me the comfort of knowing that at least one of us has behaved correctly.'

'If you'll allow a personal question, Lord Bessington, have you ever behaved incorrectly?'

'Yes. At the age of eight I brought my pony back to the stables without cooling him down and I was thrashed for it.'

'Thank you,' says Max. 'I have nothing further.'

'Hello,' says Vicky at the Coliseum Shop. 'Coliseum Shop.'

'Hi,' says Max. 'Max Lesser here. Any word from Lola?'

'Only that she's quit her job and gone away.'

'Did she say whether she . . . Did she say how she is, you know, physically?' says Max.

'All she said was what I just told you.'

'Nothing about where she was going or how long she'll be away?'

'Nothing. I have to go now.' She hangs up.

'Our child,' says Max to his mind, 'is it alive or dead?'

'I can't help you,' says his mind.

Max dials the speaking clock. 'At the third stroke,' says the clock, 'the time, sponsored by Accurist, will be fifteen thirty-three and ten seconds. Beep. Beep, etc. *Every hour wounds; the last one kills.*'

'You can say that again,' says Max.

'*Every hour wounds,*' speaks the clock; '*the last one kills.*'

LOLA LOLA

April 1997. Poole Hospital. '*Ich bin die fesche Lola*,' sings Max's mind. 'Tee-tumty-tumty-tum.'

'Ah!' says Max. 'Haunt me, Lola!'

The memory that haunts him is from February, shortly after he and Lola did the I Ching. They'd arranged to meet at his place, and when Lola arrives she says, 'Excuse me for a moment.' Then she heads for the bathroom with her Nike sports bag that she uses for an overnighter. In a few minutes she knocks three times on her side of the closed door.

'Who's there?' says Max.

'Lola Lola,' says Lola. The door opens and here she is in a black corset, frilly black knickers, suspender belt, black stockings and black high heels. She strikes a pose with feet apart, hands on hips.

'Wow,' says Max. 'Dietrich never looked this good.'

'*Ich bin die fesche Lola, der Liebling der Saison. Ich hab' ein Pianola zu Haus in mein Salon*,' sings Lola, with her upper-class English accent. 'I am the dashing Lola, the darling of the season. I have a Pianola at home in my salon.'

'Is that where you got your name?' says Max.

'Not really,' says Lola. 'I had a grandmother named Lola,

but Daddy has always been a big Dietrich fan, and when I was little he used to bounce me on his knee and sing me that song from *The Blue Angel*. He only knew the first line but he'd tumty-tum the rest and give me a kiss at the end. Actually he still sings it to me now and then.'

'With the knee ride and the kiss?' says Max.

'No, he stopped the knee rides when I was about fourteen.'

'About time, too,' says Max. 'What about the kiss?'

'Well, you know – fond parent, only child.'

'On the mouth?'

'Yes. Have you got a problem with that?'

'Maybe. I won't ask about his tongue.'

'A notable show of restraint,' says Lola. 'Would you like to help me out of this corset?'

'Yes,' says Max in his bed in Poole Hospital. The essence of Lola is feeding into him as it were intravenously. Never until now has he felt the charm of her, the strangeness, the sweetness and the pathos of her running in his veins like this. 'Lola, Lola, Lola,' he whispers.

'Did you call me?' says Nurse Laura, approaching on sturdy footsteps.

'Just talking to myself,' says Max.

32

EARTH WORK

April 1997. Max has no luck with his attempts to speak to
Lola on the telephone, nor can he find out anything about
her when he tries other people. All he has now is the absence
of Lola. This is a presence in its own right, a Lola made up
of what he can remember. And Max remembers more than
he knew. His mind gives him details of things he hadn't
been aware of noticing. The blue Guernsey, faded jeans and
denim jacket she was wearing on the day of their picnic (she
hadn't dressed warmly enough for a cold March day). The
hiking boots with the kind of wear that comes from actual
hiking. How her hair looked blowing in the wind. A dab
of mustard on her chin. An opal ring. A hand gesture. The
way she walked going up and coming down. The sky around
her. 'Primula,' she said when he asked the name of the little
yellow flowers by the path. 'Primula,' says Max in his hospital
bed. 'Primulola.'

When Max is discharged from hospital he's not yet ready
to leave Dorset. He gets a taxi to take him to Maiden Castle
and wait for him while he climbs to where he and Lola had
their picnic. First he has a look at the information boards:
an artist's impression of Maiden Castle in the Iron Age;

then HILL FORTS; MAIDEN CASTLE (maps of it in successive phases); THE NEOLITHIC AND BRONZE AGE PHASES; IRON AGE PHASES I, II, III, and IV; and AFTER THE ROMAN CONQUEST. Max backs away hastily from this glut of information that tries to get between him and the Mai Dun that was Lola's and his.

Here it is with its green and brown and tawny grasses, its eminence of centuries. Mai Dun does not impose itself on the sky, it lives with it as the sea does. Its stillness is full of life and listening with the ears of all its dead. 'Absent friends,' says Max as he (a little weak in the legs) starts up the brown path. He wishes he'd brought champagne so that he could pour a libation to those friends as Lola did. He feels that he needs all their goodwill now. Here are little white daisies and yellow primulas, this year's new flowering on the ancient earth. The grass smells sweet, like a childhood memory.

He makes his way to the inner rampart where he and Lola had their picnic. Today he doesn't see the Ark and the raven. The sky is dull and grey. Looking to the south, past the outer ramparts and ditches, he takes in the tree-lined fields and meadows undulating in easy sweeps to the blue distance. Here they sat. Here is the ribbon she tied to the grass stem. It's blue, fluttering in the same wind. It's realer than it was when she put it there, it's more than itself. 'What is it?' Max says to his mind. 'Is it that reality isn't real to me the first time around?'

'What it is,' says his mind, 'is that *you* aren't always real the first time around. Now that she's gone you'll know what she was to you. More and more.'

Max knows that he can't change anything, knows it right down to his bones. But he says to himself, 'If Lula Mae hadn't . . . If I hadn't . . . What? And here on Mai Dun, what exactly did I say, what did Lola say?'

'What's the use of going there?' says his mind. 'Let it be.'

'We said the names of the seven stars of Ursa Major,' says Max. 'We said, "Max and Lola. Lola and Max." We looked at Hale-Bopp. I said, "You seem to be good friends with the stars."

'She said, "Yes. I'm pregnant."

'I said, "Wow."

'She said, "Say more."

'I said, "Speechless." We hugged and kissed.

'She said, "So you're happy about it?"

'I said, "Like crazy."'

Max pauses, lies down with his face to the ground. He smells the earth, the ancient grasses, the summer suns, the winter rains, the cookfires of the dead.

'But then,' says Max's mind, 'in the car . . .'

'She said, "You said you're happy about it but you don't seem happy."

'I said, "It's a lot to take in."'

'Right there,' says Max's mind, 'is where you should have stopped. Skip to the part where the shit hit the fan.'

Max says, 'She said, "Wait a minute – do I smell Lula Mae Flowers again?"'

Max's mind says, 'That's where I told you to deny everything. And what did you say?'

'"I cheat but I don't lie,"' says Max. 'Then Lola said, "So you've slept with her," and I said, "I'm afraid so."'

'Because you don't lie,' says his mind. 'You just kill people with the truth.'

'Lola said, "Say more,"' says Max, '"I need to know the whole thing so this day can be complete." So I said, "She's . . ." and Lola said, "O my God. Don't say it. Say it."

'"Pregnant," I said.'

'Stop already,' says Max's mind. 'I can't bear it.'

'Now I've lost Lola,' says Max. 'And maybe she's lost the baby. Lost our child.'

'I have nothing to say,' says his mind.

33

VICTORIAN ATTITUDES

April 1997. 'Jesus,' says Lula Mae. 'You look like you've been dipped in shit three times and pulled out twice.'

'Something like that,' says Max. They're at The White Horse again, drinking pints of Bass.

'Where've you been?' says Lula Mae. 'I've been calling you and getting the answering machine for the last two and a half weeks.'

Max tells her where he's been, who said what, and what happened.

'Poor Lola!' says Lula Mae. 'Is the baby all right?'

'I don't know. I haven't been able to talk to Lola or find out anything about her.'

'So what's going to happen now?'

'I don't know.' Evasive posture.

'You're tiptoeing across that road like a possum caught in the headlights.'

Max lets a What-Can-I-Say? expression appear on his face. High overhead an aeroplane passes, trailing a banner: SAY SOMETHING, MAX.

'I'll make it easy for you,' says Lula Mae. 'You're only a little bit in love with me, no more than that. And I'm only a little bit in love with you. We've given each other a lot of pleasure. That first time at my place you recited "The Courtship of the Yonghy-Bonghy Bo" while we made love. It was weird and it was wonderful and we hadn't ever had anybody like each other before but doing it more times didn't really take us any further. You know and I know that we haven't got marriage and a family and growing old together in us. What I *do* have in me is being a single mum and doing my own thing in the place where I feel best, which is Austin.'

'That was fast. No sooner am I a father-to-be than both my kids-to-be leave me. Is this a record?'

'"There never was a horse that couldn't be rode, there never was a cowboy that couldn't be throwed."'

'True. I guess you did give me fair warning.'

'This is not a sad ending, Max – we're simply accepting that you can't pour out of a jug more than you poured into it.'

'There's no use crying over spilt milk,' says Max, 'and certainly a stitch in time saves nine.'

'There you go, and bear in mind that I'll keep you up to date with letters and photos, plus you can visit as much as you like or even move to Texas if you want to keep an eye on Victor or Victoria.'

'You've chosen a name already?'

'Well, I believe any kid of ours will be a winner, so I thought Victor for a boy and Victoria for a girl.'

Max sees, as in those stop-motion films of flowers unfolding, Victor/Victoria growing from infancy upward. He hopes the child will have Lula Mae's looks and her brains as well. Tears seem to be running down his cheeks. 'I'll help with money,' he says.

'We can work out the details later,' says Lula Mae. 'Maybe the next round should be double scotches. My shout.'

'I hear you,' says Max.

'Ah,' says a nearby drinker as Lula Mae's going-away view passes.

'I know,' says Max.

34

LEVY UNBURDENED

April 1997. Work has always been the sovereign remedy for Max. Riven as he is by guilt, shame, remorse, doubt and general funk he returns to his Moe Levy pages.

'You took your time,' says Moe.

'My time took me,' says Max. 'Be with you in a moment, got to do the epigraph.' He gets a book from the shelf and copies the following:

> Some memories are realities, and are better than anything that can ever happen to one again.
>
> Willa Cather, *My Antonia*

'If I believed that I'd give up right now,' says Moe. 'Where are we going with this?'

'Do you want to put down the dwarf or not?' says Max.

'Not if it means living in the past with nothing to look forward to,' says Moe.

'Maybe you don't deserve anything to look forward to,' says Max. 'You're not a good man.'

'So why bother with me? Why not write a nice guy for your protagonist?'

'I work with the material that comes to me and I go where it takes me,' says Max. 'Anyhow, no more dwarf, he never happened. We're scrapping whatever I've done so far. This thing now has a title: *Her Name Was Lulu.*'

'Is that the first line of a song?' says Moe.

'No,' says Max. 'Chapter One is WHEN MOE MET LULU.'

'OK,' says Moe. 'Give me good things to remember.'

'More than you deserve,' says Max.

'Maybe a little mercy along with your justice?' says Moe. 'Even bad guys can have things to look forward to.'

'All I can promise is that I'll explore the material,' says Max, and he starts typing at a pretty good rate of knots. He met Lola towards the end of December 1996 and he last saw her on the 22nd of March 1997. In those three months they spent a lot of hours together so there's plenty of material to explore for Moe and Lulu. Moe will fall in love with Lulu when he meets her at the Coliseum Shop and they'll have many pleasant days and evenings before Moe's wandering eye gets him into trouble.

As Max works, his mind is busy sorting words and pictures along with sounds, smells, and the taste and feel of everything in his times with Lola. Just as witnesses under hypnosis recall more than they think they noticed, Max finds details he hadn't remembered until now. The memories are fresh and vivid, realer than themselves. Like the ribbon on Mai Dun and the mustard on Lola's chin. There was the time in St Martin's Lane when they found the drawings of Heinrich Kley in two paperback volumes in the Dover Bookshop. Turning the pages past elephants and crocodiles on ice skates and showjumping centaurs Lola comes upon a naked giantess who is a luxurious landscape on which tiny men climb up and slide down and variously enjoy themselves. 'What do you think of that?' she says to Max.

'I've always known that women are much bigger than men,' says Max.

'Discuss,' says Lola.

'Have you ever seen the Whitbread Brewery horses parked outside The Duke of Cumberland in the New King's Road?' says Max.

'Are you going to compare women to horses?' says Lola.

'In a particular way,' says Max. 'I was passing there once while the barrels were being trundled into the cellar. It was raining and those great horses were standing there with the steam coming up off their backs. They have something prehistoric about them, something from before Coca-Cola and McDonald's and Walt Disney. That's why people want to be thought well of by horses. They give the Whitbread horses apples and lumps of sugar and they talk to them respectfully. Women have that prehistoric something also. Some men like it, others are scared by it. I like it.'

'Even though I'm smaller than a brewery horse and I'm not much good at pulling a dray?'

'You may be small in beer haulage but you're big with me,' says Max.

'Will you feed me apples and lumps of sugar?' says Lola.

'All the time,' says Max, smiling because Lola is looking very coltish in a short plaid skirt, purple tights, and fur-trimmed boots. A donkey jacket, purple muffler, and little black beret complete her outfit. Her fair hair is in a long thick plait that hangs down her back, 'if I don't eat you up first,' he says. They kiss among the Dover paperbacks. The ice-skating elephants and crocodiles whirl in their pages, long scarves streaming out behind them. The lights are lit in St Martin's Lane, the sky is dark and thick, rosy with the loom of London. Snow begins to fall. 'When it stops we can turn St Martin's Lane upside-down and make it snow again,' says Lola. 'This is what it is to be happy,' thinks Max within the memory he's typing. Lola's cheeks are like cold apples as he kisses them. He falls out of the memory with a sudden drop. No more Lola. 'Ahhh,' sighs Max.

'What a girl!' says Moe Levy. 'I love my Lulu.'

'Your Lulu!' says Max.

'It says right here,' says Moe: '"'All the time,' says Moe, smiling because Lulu is looking very coltish . . ." Hello? Are you there?'

'Where?' says Max.

'In Chapter Four,' says Moe, 'APPLES, LUMPS OF SUGAR.'

'Right,' says Max. 'I'm with you.'

'I feel as if I'm going to blow a gasket,' says Max's mind. 'Do we have to keep doing these memories?'

'What else have we got?' says Max.

'No more Lula Mae?' says his mind.

'Where've you been?' says Max. 'That's all over, she's going back to the States. She'll send photos, I'll send money.'

'And have you become wise?' says his mind.

'Not yet,' says Max.

35

LAST ORDERS

April 1997. Goodbye drinks at The White Horse. Tomorrow Lula Mae and the unborn Victor/Victoria are flying back to Texas. 'Homecoming Queen,' says Max. 'Have you ever actually been one?'

'High school and college both,' says Lula Mae with a modest smile. 'It's a dirty job but somebody's got to do it.'

'Have you told your parents you're coming?' says Max.

'Oh yes, they'll be meeting me at the airport.'

'Told them about their grandchild-to-be?'

'Not yet.'

'How do you think they'll take the news?'

'They'll open a few bottles of champagne and they'll be impatient to start spoiling him or her. I chose my parents carefully and they're my kind of people.'

'Probably a lot of jocks and ex-jocks hoping to see you again?' says Max.

'The jocks are a while back,' says Lula. 'Before you it was mostly executives.'

'I wonder who'll be next,' says Max.

Lula Mae shakes her head and takes Max's hand. 'I'm not the same as I was before I met you.'

'Definitely not,' says Max, patting her in the area of major change. He finds that he has to wipe his eyes.

'Whatever happens,' says Lula Mae, 'Victor or Victoria won't ever . . .' She also needs to wipe her eyes.

'Won't ever . . . ?' says Max.

'Call anybody but you Daddy,' says Lula Mae.

Long kiss, long embrace. 'Time for our last double scotches,' says Max.

36

FORGETFULNESS
REMEMBERED

May 1997. Max's pages are accumulating. He doesn't know
how Moe Levy's story will end but he trusts that this will be
revealed to him in the fullness of time. Moe has no complaints
at the moment. He's not a writer, he's a painter, and he's
already done a portrait and many sketches of Lulu.

Max's mind is kept busy riffling through its files as Max's
memories become Moe's life. Today he's recalling a visit to
the V & A with Lola. This will be the Moe and Lulu activity
in Chapter Nine. No title for it yet. Max's mind gives him
Lola and himself back in early February. Up the museum steps
they go, through the revolving doors and into warmth and
brightness, long spaces and echoes, years overlapped like fish
scales. Bowls and goblets, wine of shadows. Women, men,
gods and demons in stone, clay, bronze, ivory. Some with
open eyes, some with closed. Fabrics and jewels embracing
absent friends.

'Let's go to the Nehru Gallery,' says Lola. They hear music
as they approach. On a dais musicians with sitar, tabla, flute
and harmonium are playing a classical raga, far-away warm
and bright in the dark London winter. The music is not loud

but it is very wide. Max and Lola are standing in front of a display case in which they see Shiva Nataraja dancing in bronze, his hair streaming symmetrically to right and left. Dancing in a bronze ring of fire, Shiva Nataraja with his four arms, his hands with drum, with flame, with 'Fear not', with pointing to his uplifted left foot. Under his right foot is a dwarf all blackish green with patina. It has a long body, short arms and legs. Under Shiva's foot it is like an animal, something that goes on all fours. Its baby-face, is it reposeful? Max thinks it is. 'That's Apasmara Purusha,' says Lola. 'The dwarf demon called Forgetfulness.'

'Among other things,' says Max. 'Is he someone you visit often?'

'Our lives are made of memories,' says Lola. 'Everything up to the present moment, even the word now leaving my mouth, is a memory. I come here every now and then to make sure Apasmara's still under Shiva's foot.'

'He's a dangerous guy,' says Max, 'but even if he got loose he couldn't make me forget you. Fear not.'

On the page Max is typing, that's what Moe says to Lulu. 'I'd just as soon you hadn't put those words in my mouth,' says Moe to Max. 'They seem unlucky to me.'

'Be brave,' says Max. 'We've all got to take our chances.' He goes back to the beginning of the chapter and types in the title: FEAR NOT.

37

MONSTROUS VIRTUE

June 1997. Max is chugging along comfortably with Moe and Lulu. Moe and Lulu visit the National Gallery, look at the Claudes, and encounter Linda Lou Powers from Austin. Moe and Linda Lou chat briefly, she says where she works, Moe admires her going-away view and so on. Moe has no need for a research visit to Holborn so Max sends him to Blacks for a new rucksack.

'This is where you drop by Himalaya Technology and go out for lunch with Linda Lou,' says Max to Moe.

'What for?' says Moe.

'Hey,' says Max, 'don't come the innocent with me, I'm the guy who's writing you.'

'Oh, really?' says Moe. 'How often have I heard you say that your characters develop a life of their own and you go with the action that comes out of that.'

'That's all very well,' says Max, 'but if you can pass up Linda Lou you must be dead from the waist down.'

'No need to be coarse,' says Moe. 'Linda Lou is certainly attractive but Lulu is all the woman I need and all the woman I want. I've got no interest left over for anyone else.'

'My God,' says Max. 'I've created a monster. So what are you going to do now?'

'I'm going to go home and stretch a canvas,' says Moe. 'Tonight I'm starting a nude of Lulu.'

'Wonderful,' says Max. 'Do you think you're better than I am?'

'Let's just say that I think of you as a demiurge,' says Moe, 'a brute creator that gets things started but doesn't really know what to do with them, OK?'

'That a character of mine should talk to me like that!' says Max. 'How sharper than a serpent's tooth.'

'I didn't ask to be written,' says Moe.

38

A WHOLE NEW BALL GAME

June 1997. Max is utterly gobsmacked by Moe's put-down. As a writer of fiction he draws on himself, with whatever changes are required for the people he invents. They are taller or shorter than he is, braver or less brave, more honest or less, more aggressive or less. Better at sports perhaps, or talented in ways he isn't. But never before has one of them assumed the moral high ground and lectured him from there. 'What do I do now?' he asks his mind.

'Explore your material,' comes the answer.

'I always do,' says Max. 'You know that.'

'So keep doing it,' says his mind. 'You always say that if you knew how the story was going to come out you wouldn't bother writing it.'

'Give me a break,' says Max. 'This is a whole new ball game and I need time to think about it. Moe has made me so ashamed of myself. Lola is so much more than I realised. She keeps expanding like a flower unfolding. She fills my whole being with what she was to me, all that I never knew until now.'

'Ever heard the expression, "A day late and a dollar short?"'

'Yes,' says Max.

'There you have it,' says Max's mind.

39

THE BIG STORE

July 1997. Max dreams that he's in a big store. Much bigger than Harrods. Very bright. Full of all kinds of things but it isn't clear what they are. He seems to have bought something but his hands are empty. A pretty young woman in a black dress is facing him. 'Thank you for helping me choose,' says Max.

'My pleasure,' says the woman. They're looking into each other's eyes so Max kisses her. Tiny kiss, closed mouth. She smiles broadly, almost sings 'La la la.' 'If I can help you with anything else, please let me know,' she says as Max wakes up.

He looks at his hands. 'What did I buy?' he says.

40

NOAH?

July 1997. 'On March twenty-first Lola said she was pregnant,' says Max. 'She'd probably been a couple of weeks late with her period before she found out. Say she was due the first week in March, then she'd have been ovulating around the middle of February. That's when our child was conceived.'

'Right,' says his mind. 'And this is the middle of July so she's five months gone.'

'If she didn't lose the baby when we crashed,' says Max.

'I don't think she lost it,' says his mind.

'Why not?' says Max.

'It's in the nature of things that you should have two children that you'll probably never see.'

'That's hard.'

'That's your life. Get used to it.'

That night Max dreams the Ark drifting through rain and storm and dark of night. The sky clears and it's the dawn of a new day. Here's the Ark stranded on the mountains of Ararat. Here's the rainbow sign of the covenant. The little door up near the peak of the Ark's roof opens and Max sees a face. The face of a child, a boy. The boy's face comes closer, closer. His eyes grow bigger, bigger. 'Noah?' says Max.

'Daddy?' says the Noah child.

41

NO ANSWER

July 1997. Max turns on Fujitsu/Siemens, says, 'Take me to
Moe Levy's place.' Fujitsu/Siemens shrugs, hums a little, and
sets him down in a desolation where the policemen walk in
fours when they (rarely) go there. Sodden mattresses, rusty
bedsprings, and broken prams litter the concrete yard. The
lift doesn't work, which is just as well since it seems to be
used as a toilet. Max walks slowly up five flights, pausing to
rest from time to time. A long balcony overlooks the yard
and he goes from door to door (all of them covered with
graffiti) until he finds one with the name Levy under the bell.
He rings but the bell doesn't work. He knocks but there's
no answer. He knocks again and keeps it up until he hears
footsteps. 'Whaddaya want?' says a voice. Male? Female? Max
is unsure.

'I want to talk to Moe,' he says.

'Not here,' says the voice. The footsteps recede.

'Where is he then?' says Max.

No answer.

'When's he coming back?' says Max.

No answer.

'I don't understand it,' says Max to himself. 'What's he doing in a dump like this?'

No answer.

42

EVERY HOUR

November 1997. Max has not attempted any communication with Moe Levy since July. He wishes he'd never gone to that dreadful council flat, he'll certainly never go there again. He doesn't feel too comfortable with Fujitsu/Siemens any more. He doesn't check his e-mail or turn on the modem. Once in a while he scribbles something in longhand and he keeps a clipboard handy with yellow sheets of A4 but the top page says nothing except:

3 BOTTLES OF RED
CRISPS, OLIVES

There is a poem by Walter de la Mare, 'Goodnight'. It begins:

Look thy last on all things lovely every hour

This line has got into Max's head as:

Look thy last on Lola lovely every hour

It's in his brain like one of those pop tunes that won't go away and Max is sick and tired of it.

Lula Mae is also in his thoughts. He's had short notes from her in her rounded and loopy handwriting. No Everest Technology printouts, the notes call up Lula Mae's roundnesses, the generosity with which she gave herself. Photos of her, full-length frontal and profile. The pregnancy's been coming along nicely, no problems. She's had ultrasounds but she's asked not to be told the baby's sex. 'I know it's going to be a boy,' she says, 'and I don't want to hear it from anyone else. Victor feels comfortable inside me and I love him dearly. He's got a kick like a mule. I've been reading Edward Lear to him, I want to start him off right. I'm staying with my parents for the time being and I'm still with Everest. I'll take my maternity leave when I'm closer to my time. They have a good medical plan so Victor and I will have the best of care. Thanks for the check. Give my regards to Clowed. Love XXX, Lula Mae.'

Max imagines Victor reclining comfortably in Lula Mae's womb, listening to her pleasant voice with his feet up, shaking his head thoughtfully from time to time as he takes in the tragicomic histories of the Yonghy-Bonghy Bo, the Jumblies, and the Dong with a luminous Nose. 'Lucky kid,' he says. He wipes his eyes and blows his nose.

'He'd be luckier with two parents,' says his mind.

'Lula Mae could have stayed here,' says Max. 'But Austin is her homeplace and that's where she wants to be. And London has become my homeplace. So there we are with an ocean between us.'

'Is there something in you that doesn't want life to be simple?' says his mind.

'I'd *like* it to be simple,' says Max. 'I just don't know how to manage it.'

43

AFTER THE FLOOD

28 November 1997. '*Shalom,*' says Lord Bessington as the nurse shows him his grandchild, born at 03:15 this morning.

'Really,' says his wife, 'he doesn't look all that Jewish.'

'That's only because he's not circumcised,' says the Lord of Appeal in Ordinary. 'When he's decently covered there'll be no mistaking that the stork who dropped him off was wearing a yarmulka.'

The new boy, who is large (nine pounds, two ounces), well made, and with an abundance of black hair, squints at Lord Bessington, screws up his face, and lets out a yell.

'You know you love him,' says Lady Bessington. 'He's beautiful. Look at the intelligence in his eyes.'

'I don't doubt that he's clever,' says Lord Bessington. 'He's already demonstrated a talent for self-advancement.'

'Come on,' says Lady Bessington. 'His father is a well-established writer. His Charlotte Prickles books are classics. I'm sure his genes are nothing to be ashamed of.'

'In my experience,' says Lord Bessington, 'writers can be relied on for just the sort of moral unreliability demonstrated by this chap's father. Our grandchild was born at quarter past three in the morning, so he's already keeping late hours.'

'For better or worse, the father's name on the birth certificate is Max Lesser,' says Lady Bessington. 'But don't forget that our Lola's his mum. We've got to be genetically open-minded. I have to say I'm optimistic.'

Lola takes the baby for a feed. He applies himself to her breast like a connoisseur. A hungry one. Lola's looking wonderful. She had an easy birth (natural) and she's enjoying her son's pleasure.

'What are you going to call him?' says Lady Bessington.

'Noah,' says Lola. 'Noah Bessington.'

'May he see rainbows,' says her father before he can stop himself.

'Are you sure you don't want to tell Max?' says Lady Bessington.

'I begrudge Max Lesser even the memory of what we had,' says Lola. 'I'd like him to forget he ever knew me.'

'His name is on the birth certificate because I play by the rules,' says Lord Bessington. 'So he *does* have certain legal rights if he chooses to claim them.'

'I'll deal with that when the time comes,' says Lola. 'But for the present he's not to be told anything at all.'

'Tsuck, tsuck,' says little Noah. He knows a rainbow when he tastes one.

44

SYNCHRONICITY

December 1997. WHALING VOYAGE BY ONE ISHMAEL. BLOODY BATTLE IN AFGHANISTAN. Synchronicity! Nobody owns the passing moment. It isn't exclusively yours or anyone else's. This very moment (already past) as you read these words is shared by every creature living and dead, by every stone and leaf and door, by the trackless seas, the deeps of space, and whatever vast and trunkless legs of stone may be standing out in the desert.

The naked baby in the photograph, though quite new, is well developed and beautifully finished in every detail. Genetically a good job. Blue eyes and blond hair. 'My son,' says Max. 'My son the gentile.' He wipes his eyes, blows his nose.

'Victor Maxim Flowers was born at 03:15 on November 28th,' says Lula Mae's letter, 'William Blake's birthday (I looked up the date in the almanac). He weighed nine pounds, two ounces. We did natural childbirth all the way and he came out like a real pro, looking good. I had an easy time, as I'd expected, and you and I, Max dear, have a beautiful son. A Sagittarius. May his arrows always hit their mark.' More eye-wiping, nose-blowing. 'Your name is on the birth certificate and Victor will always know who his daddy is. All babies start out with blue eyes so we don't know yet what color his will be. As you can see, he's built like a fullback, and his grandad, who was one himself, has already given him a small Texas Longhorn T-shirt to grow into. If I can get him away from my mother now and then I'll make sure that his Maxness is encouraged and given room to grow. I have known one or two fullbacks in my time (not counting Daddy), and although Vic seems to have my looks I hope he has your brains. Kind of. Now that he's outside me I can see him when I read to him and that makes it more interesting. Today when we did the "Yonghy-Bonghy Bo" he said, "Ah!" sympathetically when we got to the turtle ride with its "sad primeval motion/ Towards the sunset Isles of Boshen". Maybe it was gas but nobody can tell me he hasn't absorbed the mood of that poem from all those prenatal readings. I'm breastfeeding, and from the way he takes to it I may not wean him (or myself) for quite a long time. Maybe Everest will let me work from home so I can fit my client visits into my own schedule. I hope you're closer to Page One. Our next reading here will be *Charlotte Prickles, Lollipop Lady*. Love XXX, Lula Mae.'

Max looks at the photograph again and feels himself moved back in time to see, through the eyes of his father, himself as a naked baby. Max was named after Maxim Gorky. Max's father, Alexander, had seen Gorky's play, *The Lower Depths*, and had read it many times. 'To write like this,' he said, 'is to see the whole world in what you look at.' Alexander Lesser was a homeopath. Max was born at the Hahnemann Hospital in Philadelphia, which was named after the founder of homeopathy. His father sat his patients at an optical device on which they propped their chins while he examined their irises and explained why their circulation was bad or their bones ached. He took Max to the pharmacy where his prescriptions were filled. It was cool and dark. It smelled like midnight gardens, dusty caravans, secret caves. There were tall cabinets of many drawers with white china knobs. From the blue lettering on the white porcelain label plates Max copied some of the names: *valerian*; *veronica*; *calendula*; *melissa*; *belladonna atropa*; *primula*. They were like the names of beautiful women, he liked the feel of them in his mouth. These magical ingredients were dispensed in little bottles with complex instructions. Alexander Lesser had loyal patients who claimed to be helped by the medicines and came back again and again. Max too, when feeling not quite right, propped his chin on the iridology device and was given little bottles and instructions.

'Think of it,' his father used to say – 'in a thousandfold dilution, the memory of a single drop of medicine persists and works its cure. Only the memory! In a single cell of a human being is the memory of the whole design. In each of us is the memory, however inaccessible, of the beginning of the universe. We are the memory of the dust of stars.' He would press his forehead against Max's. 'In you,' he said, 'there must be memories inherited from me. I know I have these from my father – black trees, the smell of snow, the sound of cossacks. Ravens.'

Remembering his words, Max sees again Noah's Ark stranded on the mountains of Ararat behind the boiler. He sees the raven loop the loop and fly away and wonders if Victor will remember it. 'A single drop,' says Max. He recalls that when he had chicken pox and measles his mother called Dr Farber, a regular GP.

45

NOT A RETREAT

December 1997. 'Diamond Heart,' says the brochure, 'is not a retreat. It is a centre of dynamic calm in which mind and spirit gather energy for the next forward move.' On offer are yoga, tai chi, feng shui, and Zen disciplines including meditation, gardening, flower arrangement, archery, snooker, and poker. Vegetarian, kosher, and halal cuisine. Acupuncture, reflexology, aromatherapy, and homeopathic medicine. Tuition in classical Indian music with Hariprasad and Indira Ghosh. The photograph shows Mr Ghosh sitting crosslegged with a sitar. He's wearing a proper sitar-playing outfit just like Ravi Shankar. He looks like someone you could trust.

Diamond Heart, established two years ago, has given a new lease of life to the defunct herring port of Port Malkie on the Firth of Moray. The harbour is almost empty, stretching out its arms to the past. The tide comes in, goes out around coastal features known locally as Kirsty's Knowe, Teeny Titties, and Deil's Hurdies. The wind sighs in the grasses. The pebbles rattle in the tidewash, the sea-shapen rocks abide. There are plenty of gulls, shags, and cormorants but no herring. Port Malkie, however, now buzzes with new businesses supplying goods and services to Diamond Heart.

Diamond Heart is not cheap. The one thing its varied clientele have in common is that they can all afford it. There are ageing hippies, youthful rebels, stressed-out executives, ex-husbands and ex-wives, broken-down pop stars, actors in the throes of expanding consciousness, and everything between. Cannabis is not compulsory. The Diamond Heart complex has many large and small dome-shaped buildings (called tholoi in the brochure) overlooking the sea. Lola and little Noah occupy a medium-sized tholos which is designated as a family unit. It has a small but adequate galley and is equipped with a washing machine, dryer, and dishwasher. The town is geared up to deliver everything necessary to the residents of Diamond Heart twenty-four hours a day. Although only recently arrived, Lola settles in quickly and is already known among the other residents as the E-type from Belgravia.

As soon as possible she goes to sign up for private tuition with Hariprasad Ghosh. When she shows up at his studio he's sitting crosslegged on a Kelim. He's wearing jeans and a green sweatshirt on which is a gold-tinted photograph of a Kola bronze of Shiva Nataraja with the words DIAMOND HEART arcing over Shiva's ring of fire. Mr Ghosh is a man of slight physique with a face that makes it difficult to guess his age. When he stands up to greet her she feels as if he can read her mind. His bare feet look ingenuous but not naive. Cushions and hassocks lie about. There's a long table with various instruments on it, sheet music and music paper with handwritten notation. Lola recognises sitar, tabla, flutes. She's been thinking sitar but now another instrument is talking to her. 'What's that one?' she says, pointing.

'That's a sarod,' says Mr Ghosh. 'Like the sitar, it's a thirteenth-century instrument. Eight main strings and this one has sixteen resonating strings. The body is hollowed-out wood but the top is leather and the fingerboard is metal. You use a coconut-shell plectrum. It's not like the sitar, it hasn't got any frets. You have to find the notes by yourself, as with a violin. Because it is more difficult to learn than the sitar it is not so popular here. It requires a good musical ear and hard concentration.'

Lola takes the sarod in her hands, feels the weight of it. It's the instrument Clint Eastwood would choose, it's the .357 magnum. 'This is the one I want to learn,' she says.

'Are you a musician?' says Mr Ghosh.

'I play the piano a little.'

'The sarod requires great dedication and patience,' says Mr Ghosh. 'It will take a lot of time.'

'I've got the time, and I want lessons every day.'

'It is my wife who teaches sarod,' says Mr Ghosh. 'If you wish to go ahead with this, she will see you tomorrow.'

'A woman,' says Lola. 'Yes, I'd like to be taught by a woman.'

'The fee is forty pounds an hour. You want to do this every day?'

'Yes.'

The next day Lola loads Noah into his pram and returns to the studio to meet Indira Ghosh. She is a small woman in a red sari. She has a red bindi on her forehead. Her face is round, and at the first glance childlike. But it is the face of a child who cannot be fooled by anybody or anything. She smiles when she sees Noah and greets him with a little bow. 'What is your child's name?' she asks.

'Noah.'

'A good name.' Hearing this, Noah smiles.

Lola lifts the carry-cot out of the undercarriage and puts

it on the floor so that Noah can see her. Mrs Ghosh notes this and nods approvingly. 'You wish to learn the sarod?'

'Yes,'

'Why?'

'I want to be able to compose a raga of my own,' says Lola, 'and I know that it must come through familiarity with a classical instrument.'

'Ah,' says Mrs Ghosh. She shakes her head. 'This is not the way to begin. You are putting yourself ahead of the music, the lesser ahead of the greater. Humility is required here.'

'Forgive me. I have an arrogant mouth but I am truly humble.'

Mrs Ghosh looks at her as if she, like her husband, can read Lola's mind. 'Why the sarod? Why not the sitar, which is less difficult?'

'When I saw the sarod, it spoke to me,' says Lola. 'Something in me wants to make music with this instrument.'

Mrs Ghosh looks sceptical. 'You may have formed an opinion of the Diamond Heart Centre,' she says. 'It is after all a commercial enterprise. There is a demand for Zen snooker and Zen poker so those disciplines are taught here. My husband and I are not commercial. We have to make a living but we are here to introduce those who have ears for it to the spiritual essence of Indian classical music.'

'I understand,' says Lola.

'In this there is a tradition,' says Mrs Ghosh. 'It is called *gurushisyia parampara*. Do you know what that is?'

'No.'

'If you accept me as a teacher I become your guru. I become as a parent to you and must have your total trust and respect the same as your mother and father. And I must give the same love and education to you, the shisyia, as to my own child. For the shisyia there must be total surrender to the guru. And the guru must repay this trust with teaching that will guide and nurture the disciple in every way. This is something that will take years and it is a big commitment for both of us. Your son will already be starting school before you can think of composition. Will you be here that long? Do you have the dedication and the years to give this?'

Lola feels as if she's standing on a mountaintop. All around her is the sky. 'Yes,' she says.

'Then let us begin,' says Mrs Ghosh. She takes up the sarod and assumes the playing position on the Kelim. The woman and the instrument become one, as compact and contained as a Tanagra figurine. She plays a scale, singing the notes as she sounds them: 'Sa, Re, Ga, Ma, Pa, Dha, Ni.' In the acoustically dry room the sound of the sarod is surprisingly full and commanding. Mrs Ghosh's voice, low and unforced, seems a quietly resounding string of the instrument.

'Ah!' says Noah.

'It helps if you sing as you play,' says Mrs Ghosh. 'Because music is created in the mind before it comes from the instrument and the singing helps you to imagine it. The instrument is made by man; man has given it a voice, but our voice is from God, and through it we can learn a lot. Once you start getting the hang of the notes, then you bring the embellishments into your playing.' The sarod sounds again, and with it her voice and the voice of what lives in her. Lola is transported. What she hears puts her in a place she's never been before. Tears well up in her eyes. She is humbled, left with nothing to say.

'Ah!' says Noah.

'Good,' says Mrs Ghosh. 'I see that both you and Noah are hearing what there is to hear. I think your son is hungry.'

Lola puts Noah to her breast and he shows that he is indeed hungry.

'As your breast is to Noah, so must this music be to you,' says Mrs Ghosh. 'We will continue tomorrow. You may call me Indira.'

'Thank you,' says Lola. 'Would it be possible to borrow the sarod so that I can begin to get the feel of it?'

'No,' says Indira. 'You cannot borrow this one and you must not buy one. At this point you are not to touch the sarod except in our lessons. From the very beginning, your hands and your mind must only do what is correct.'

'Is there a book I can get to help me learn the positions of the notes?'

Again Mrs Ghosh shakes her head. 'I will teach you the positions of the notes. If you want a book, get *Buddhist Wisdom Books, The Diamond Sutra; The Heart Sutra*, translated by Edward Conze. There are several copies in the library here and they might have it in the shop as well.'

Lola and Noah are off to the library then. It's dome-shaped but the straight shelves are chords to the arcs of the circle, so that in plan they form a hexagon. The endless wall is white, the shelves, floors, tables and chairs are stripped pine. There are only three other people there besides the librarian. No one is smoking but the reek of cannabis hangs in the air. Noah's nose twitches a little but he's not too bothered. A tall thin man with a scraggly beard and a prominent Adam's apple comes over to Lola. He's wearing a red poncho striped with black and yellow. 'Hi,' he says. 'I'm Poncho.'

'Hi,' says Lola. 'Lola.' His handshake is wetter than she'd like.

Poncho sniffs her. 'You smell milky,' he says. 'Can I have some?'

'Go away,' says Lola. She leaves him standing there with his ardent Adam's apple and goes to the shelves.

'In *Grapes of Wrath* a young woman suckles an old man,' says Poncho. 'It's a beautiful scene.'

'There's a good suckling scene in *Les Valseuses*,' says a sturdy young woman in a T-shirt and jeans. The T-shirt says NE WAY IS OK. 'It's with a young man who can't get it up temporarily because he's been shot in the crotch. He's hoping it'll turn him on but it doesn't.'

'You have a kind T-shirt,' says Poncho. 'Let me know if you start lactating.'

'You could have a long wait,' says the sturdy young woman (her name is Morwen), 'but I'll bottle-feed you if you like.'

'Your tholos or mine?' says Poncho as they leave the library.

There's still a reader left at one of the tables. This is an OK-looking young man in jeans and a wordless T-shirt. He shakes his head and says to Lola, 'There's a lot of emptiness around here but I haven't found the form yet.'

'Maybe emptiness *is* the form,' says Lola.

'You sound very advanced,' says the young man. 'Have you been here before?'

'No,' says Lola, 'but I'm a quick study.'

'You're reading this for the first time then?' he shows her his book which is *Buddhist Wisdom Books*; *The Diamond Sutra*; *The Heart Sutra*.

'Not reading it at all. I came here to borrow a copy.'

'I'll show you where they live. I'm Mick.' He offers his hand.

'Lola,' says Lola. Handshake, dryer than the last one. Mick guides her to an empty space in the shelves. 'Emptiness,' he says. 'They're all out. Take this one – I can do without the book – I need time to think about what I've read so far.'

'Thanks, I can probably buy a copy at the shop,' says Lola. Mick puts on his jacket. 'Mind if I walk with you?' he says.

'Not at all.' The short December day has become twilight. The lamps on the pathways are pinky-orange globes set close to the ground so that the sky begins at shoulder height. Shadows drift past them. No one is singing. Cecil Court and St Martin's Lane will be bustling with Christmas shoppers now, the Coliseum Shop will be full. Lola imagines Haydn on the speakers, *The Creation* perhaps. 'Destiny woman,' murmurs Lola.

'What?' says Mick.

'Nothing. I murmur to myself a lot.'

The shop, although not Christmassy, is doing a brisk business in books, prints, posters, postcards, playing cards, CDs, videotapes, T-shirts, sweatshirts, baseball caps (all with the Diamond Heart logo), trainers, sandals, judo, karate, and tai chi outfits, jock straps, sports bras, first-aid kits, sports bags, snooker cues, baseballs, baseball bats and gloves, softballs, saris, kimonos, fans, fishing rods, cameras, binoculars, sunglasses, wooden flutes, various drums, candles, incense, hookahs, hand-carved Krishnas, Ganeshas, Shaktis, brass Shiva Natarajas in three sizes, model tholoi, Diamond Heart snowstorms, organic treacle brittle, Diamond Heart rock, and so on.

Lola is told that *Buddhist Wisdom Books* is out of print so she borrows the library copy that Mick offers. She buys *The Raga Guide* (which includes four CDs), and a boxed set of five All India Radio Archival Release CDs of the late Ustad Allauddin Khan Sahib on the sarod.

'That's a lot of sarod,' says Mick.

'I need a lot,' says Lola. She says good-night to Mick,

wheels Noah home, changes him, orders in blinis from Diamond Heart Kosher Takeaway, and hooks herself up to her personal CD player and Disc One of *The Raga Guide*. *Abhogi* is the first raga, suitable for early night (21:00 to 00:00).

46

MAKING IT DARK

December 1997. Lola dreams that she's standing on the Embankment, looking up at the Albert Bridge. She takes aim with the sarod and begins to shoot out the lights.

'You're making it dark,' says a man's voice behind her.

'They can always get more,' says Lola.

47

FORM AND EMPTINESS

December 1997. At 02:00 Noah's lusty demand for room
service wakes Lola and she gives him the breast. As always she
smiles in pleased astonishment at this complete small person
who has come out of her. Feeding him is her delight. His
satisfaction makes her proud. Still wakeful when he's replete,
she makes herself a cup of rosehip tea and picks up *Buddhist
Wisdom Books*. The much-used copy falls open at *The Heart
Sutra*, page 81. Drawn to the lines in bold type, she reads:

> **Here, O Sariputra. Form is emptiness and the very
> emptiness is form; emptiness does not differ from
> form, form does not differ from emptiness; whatever
> is form, that is emptiness, whatever is emptiness,
> that is form, the same is true of feelings, perceptions,
> impulses and consciousness.**

Lola feels that she has been entered by these words that
she cannot take in. 'Well,' she says, 'maybe understanding
is non-understanding and the very non-understanding is
understanding, right?' She feels the unknown meaning of
the words opening in her like a lotus blossom. She's never

seen a lotus blossom but her mind gives her a convincing image.

The unknown meaning feels pretty good but Lola would actually like to know it if possible so she makes an effort. Noah is beautifully formed. Is that emptiness? 'Do me a favour!' she says. Max's love for her had form that turned out to be empty. The emptiness had the form of an affair with Lula Mae who was very well formed. The girl from Texas might have been empty to begin with but Max put a bun in her oven and her form got bulgy. Lola's form also got bulgy from Max's emptiness. At this point Lola finds her eyes closing but she flips the pages back towards the beginning where her eye lights on a single line of bold type:

Mindfully fixing his attention in front of him.

She likes the sound of that. Conze's explanation follows in ordinary type, beginning with:

> Preparatory to entering into a trance, the Buddha fixes his attention on the breath which is in front of him.

'Interesting!' says Lola. 'Of course that's nothing for non-Buddhas to try at home.' Nevertheless, she mindfully fixes her attention on the breath in front of her and breathes it in. Now the scene before her eyes, the interior of her dome, begins to curl at the edges. Like a photograph held over a flame. What's happening?

This: a dwarf black as ebony with a long body, very short arms and legs, large head, big ugly baby-face. Looks like something that goes on all fours. Apasmara Purusha, demon of Forgetfulness. Lola gasps, slaps herself in the face. Apasmara's gone. Did she imagine him? Or did she only imagine that she imagined him? She puts on her headphones and listens to the raga *Adana*, depicted in a *ragamala* from Mewar (Plate 1 in *The Raga Guide*) as an ascetic seated on a tiger skin, sometimes identified as Kama, the god of love. Appropriate for late night (00:00 to 03:00).

48

NOT SO FAST

January 1998. Christmas and New Year have come and gone without Lola's participation in any festivities outside her dome. People were singing and snogging and throwing up all around Diamond Heart but she confined herself to a private two-person celebration in which she drank a couple of glasses of champagne by way of bringing in the New Year with Noah. 'Rainbows!' was her toast. He smiled, possibly anticipating some jollification in his milk.

In the fortnight since her first lesson Lola has been thinking constantly of the sarod. That fretless fingerboard is always in her mind. Every night, before or after other dreams, she sees in dreams her hands on the instrument, hears music she cannot remember. Now she sits crosslegged in the studio holding the sarod and facing Indira.

'Shisyia,' says Indira, 'let me hear the scale please.'

Lola sees her left hand on the fingerboard, her right hand holding the plectrum. 'Sa, Re, Ga, Ma, Pa, Dha, Ni,' she sings as the sarod goes up the scale.

'Stop,' says Indira before Lola can come down the scale. Lola waits in silence to be told what she's done wrong. 'This instrument in your hands is not a machine-gun,' says Indira.

'You are firing off the notes like bullets and your singing is without heart. Even the smallest act, even the tuning of the sarod, must be done in the proper spirit of devotion. Let yourself always be the true vessel for the music that comes through you. Move your mind away from all bad thoughts, let it be clear and peaceful. The scale again, please. Not so fast this time. Listen to the sounds that are coming from you.'

Lola tries to clear her mind. She can't do it. Her mind is a kaleidoscope of sounds and images. She tries to bypass these as she goes up the scale again.

'What I hear is tension,' says Indira. 'Put down the sarod. For the rest of this lesson we'll do breathing exercises.'

49

FROG HOLLOW ROAD

January 1998. Max writes:

CHARLOTTE PRICKLES ON FROG HOLLOW
ROAD
Cars went very fast on Frog Hollow Road. Many hedgehogs never reached the other side. Charlotte Prickles
put up a sign that said HEDGEHOG CROSSING –
SLOW DOWN. But it was a very small sign and it was
written in Hedgehog. Even if they saw it, drivers could
not read it.

'Are you sitting comfortably?' says Max's mind.
'No,' says Max.
'That's not a very cosy opening,' says his mind. 'Could
do better?'
'OK,' says Max. He starts again:

The big hand of the clock is at twelve.
The little hand is at three.
It is three o'clock in the afternoon.
It is bedtime at the Frog Hollow Orphanage.

Charlotte Prickles reads the little hedgehogs a bedtime story. She reads *The Hog in the Bog*. Then all the little hedgehogs kneel by their beds and say their prayers. They pray that they will reach the other side of the road when they go out this evening.

'Do we want to bring in real danger?' says Max's mind.

'Hedgehogs lead dangerous lives,' says Max.

'Whom do they pray to?' says his mind.

'I don't know,' says Max. 'Big Spikey, the hedgehog in the sky?'

'Let's bypass that for now,' says his mind. 'Continue.'

Max writes:

> Charlotte Prickles kisses each one.
> She tucks them all in.
> She takes up her darning basket and
> she darns all the socks with holes.

'I like that,' says Max's mind. 'That's cosy.'

Max continues:

> Then Charlotte goes to sleep.
> She has a strange dream and wakes up.
> She does not wake the orphans.
> She goes outside and sees the moon.
> It is a full moon.
> The moon is the colour of pale honey.
> Charlotte tastes the moon with her eyes.
> She tastes it with her mouth.
> The sweetness of it makes her sad.

'Why does the sweetness of the moon make her sad?' says Max's mind.

'The basic hedgehog condition is sadness,' says Max. 'Charlotte is thinking of how many hedgehogs have tasted the sweetness of the moon, all of them gone in the whisper of the trees and the rustling of the years.'

'Whoa, boy,' says Max's mind. 'This kind of thinking is not going to get Charlotte all the way to the bank.'

Max ignores this and carries on:

> Charlotte sees the moonlit trees.
> She sees the white road.
> She hears the rushing of cars.
> She sees the headlights.
> She smells the night.

'Where are we going with this?' says Max's mind. 'Is she thinking of crossing the road? There's an awful lot of traffic right now.'

'The moon is kind of pulling her,' says Max.

'What's on the other side of the road anyhow?' says his mind.

'Maybe she's just going to the shops,' says Max.

'Doesn't sound that way,' says his mind.

'Maybe things are better on the other side,' says Max.

'Steady on,' says his mind. 'Charlotte sounds as if she's stoned. I don't think she's in a fit state to cross the road. After all, we don't want her to get flat.'

'*I'm* flat,' says Max. 'I'm a flat orphan.'

'That's no reason to piss on your meal ticket,' says his mind. 'Leave this for now, we can come back to it another time.'

'I keep looking for another time,' says Max. 'But this seems to be the only one there is.'

50

THE NEW RUCKSACK

February 1998. 'Pardon the expression,' says Max's mind, 'but do you think we might be flogging a dead hedgehog?'

'Watch your mouth,' says Max.

'I was only speaking in a manner of speaking,' says his mind. 'Of course Charlotte's not dead. But could it be that she needs a little time to regroup, reprickle, whatever? Why not leave Frog Hollow Road for the time being and catch up with Moe Levy?'

'I don't think he likes me,' says Max.

'No harm in trying, is there?'

'There could be,' says Max. 'OK,' he says to Fujitsu/Siemens, 'let's go back to where we left off with Moe.'

Fujitsu/Siemens suppresses a laugh and puts up the heading for Chapter Twelve, THE NEW RUCKSACK. 'What's that?' says Max.

'Moe was going to Blacks for a new rucksack,' says his mind, 'and you wanted him to stop by Linda Lou's office and take her out to lunch and so on. But he didn't want to. He's being faithful to Lulu.'

'He thinks he's better than I am,' says Max.

'What did you expect?' says his mind. 'It's not unusual for

a fictional character to be a better man than the guy who wrote him.'

'OK,' says Max, 'I'll grovel as necessary. Where is he?'

'Here,' says his mind. Max finds himself on a road, way out in the middle of nowhere, fields on either side. It's like that scene in *North by Northwest* where Cary Grant is being chased by the crop-duster plane. Heat waves shimmering off the road, everything dry, everything flat. No gas station or any place where a cold beer might be available. Far up ahead Max sees a lone figure walking away from him. 'Yo!' Max shouts. 'Moe?' The figure doesn't turn, doesn't stop. Max runs to catch up with him. It's Moe all right, with his new rucksack on his back. 'Stop!' gasps Max.

'What for?' says Moe without stopping.

'We need to talk,' says Max.

'Maybe *you* do,' says Moe. 'I don't.'

'You and your superior tone,' says Max. 'Without me you'd be nothing.'

'Oh, really?' says Moe. 'Let's just see what *you* are without *me*, shall we?'

'Wait,' says Max. 'Give me a break. I'm sorry I misjudged you with that Linda Lou business. We'll do it your way – no Linda Lou.' He suddenly remembers his visit to Moe's council flat. 'And I'm sorry about that awful estate where you live.'

'I don't live there any more,' says Moe.

'The whole thing's very confusing,' says Max. 'I never wrote you into that flat.'

'Who did then?' says Moe. 'When you wanted me to take Linda Lou to lunch I said that I was going home to stretch a canvas. Home was a house in Fulham when we started, but when I got home that day it turned out to be what you saw when you came looking for me later.'

'I honestly don't know how that happened,' says Max. 'Somehow I lost the continuity thread.'

'Right,' says Moe. 'And when you lost it, that estate happened by default. Without any thought on your part, it grew out of your mental and moral squalor like a boil. I'm better off homeless.'

'Moe!' says Max. 'Please! I'll write you back into Fulham, I'll give you a skylight studio, whatever you want. I can't tell you how sorry I am!'

Moe stops and turns a pitying look on Max. 'I'm sorry too, because I just can't work with you. I suppose you'll eventually find somebody who'll say the words and do the things you want and you'll put some kind of a story together but it's time for me to say goodbye.'

'Where are you going?' says Max.

'Back where I came from,' says Moe. He begins to spin and he keeps spinning faster and faster until he becomes a dim and blurry dust-devil.

Max feels his head going round as he spins too. He falls to the ground and everything goes black.

51

JOIE DE VIVRE

February 1998. 'Let's go, champ,' says Max's mind. It shakes him gently and breaks into song. '"Just pick yourself up, dust yourself off, and start all over again."'

'Now I know why people lose their minds,' says Max.

'You don't want to lose me,' says his mind. 'I only want what's best for you.'

'And what's that?' says Max.

'I can't say. I'll know it when I see it.'

'You're no better off than I am,' says Max. 'So where's all this cheerfulness coming from?'

'You always keep a little *joie de vivre* stashed away, remember?' says his mind. 'So I thought this might be a good time to open a can.'

'That won't help,' says Max. 'I'm an orphan father and I can't write. Charlotte Prickles has gone strange and Moe Levy fired me. I don't feel real any more.'

'Now we're getting somewhere,' says his mind. 'When you felt real you weren't. Now you're a two-time loser and probably a two-time father and you've got two No Page Ones. Get real with that. Feel it inside you.'

'Shit,' says Max.

'You're boring me,' says his mind. 'You think Edward Lear wasn't feeling lousy when he wrote "The Courtship of the Yonghy-Bonghy Bo"? But he got real with it, and the base metal of that reality was transmuted into the gold of art.'

'Hang on,' says Max, 'I want to make a note not to write that down.'

'OK, smartass,' says his mind. 'Do it your way. But don't come crying to me any more. Be a fucking man.'

'I've *been* that,' says Max. 'That's how I got where I am today.' He pulls himself together and thinks about his latest attempts at Page One. 'Charlotte Prickles had a strange dream,' he says. 'I wonder what it was.' He nudges Fujitsu/Siemens out of its screen saver of flying toasters and types:

THE STRANGE DREAM OF
CHARLOTTE PRICKLES

'Charlotte,' says Max, 'talk to me.'

'I had a dream,' says Charlotte.

'Right,' says Max. 'Go on.'

'"I had a dream,"' sings Charlotte, '"You had one too. Mine was the best dream because it was of you."'

'Stop kidding around, Charlotte,' says Max. 'I'm serious. You had a strange dream. What was it?'

'I'm trying to remember,' says Charlotte. She goes quiet for a long time, looking inward. 'There was moonlight on a river. The full moon reflected in the water, in the glimmers of the water in the night. Strange moonlight, not from now. Moonlight from long ago. The sound of a fish jumping. Close but far away, far away in time.'

'Go on,' says Max.

'That's all that comes to me now,' says Charlotte. 'Maybe

I'll have that dream again and I'll remember more next time. If I do I'll let you know.'

'Thanks, Charlotte,' says Max. 'I'd be very grateful.'

52

MORE DARK THAN LIGHT

March 1998. The vernal equinox again. Max feels it inside him. The world of it. He sees Lola pull up in the E-type. Sees the names and arrows large in front of them, small behind them. Sees her ribbon fluttering on the grass stem on Mai Dun. Tastes the Cristal and her mouth. Smells her skin, her hair, her breath as she names the stars of Ursa Major. In the evening he steps outside with a starfinder and a printout of the constellation from an astronomy website. He finds Ursa Major and reads off the seven names: 'Alkaid, Mizar, Alioth, Megrez, Phecda, Merak, Dubhe.' His throat aches. He goes back into the house, gets a bottle of Glenfiddich and a glass. He walks over to the common, looks up at the stars again. 'Absent friend,' he says, and pours some whisky on the grass. Pause. 'Absent child?' he pours some more. Then he pours himself a large one and drinks it standing there. 'Will there ever be anything,' he says, 'to equal what I've lost?'

No answer.

53

ABSENT FRIEND

March 1998. The evening of the vernal equinox at Diamond Heart. Morwen and a few friends are dancing naked around a fire on the hill called Kirsty's Knowe. Others are marking the occasion indoors with candles, incense, chanting, musical improvisation and whatever stimulants come to hand. For the Zen poker and snooker players the night is always longer than the day even when it's not. They carry on as usual.

Mick has invited Lola to look at the stars with him but she has declined. She steps outside her dome with a bottle of champagne, looks up at the sky, locates Ursa Major. She uncorks the bottle, says, 'Absent friend,' and pours a little on the ground. She goes back inside, pours herself a glass, raises it to the sleeping Noah, and drinks it down.

54

PRICKLES OF MEMORY

June 1998. Although Max is sometimes free and easy with Charlotte Prickles he never forgets that she's his meal ticket. Having had no Page One these many weeks he is very careful when he visits her again. 'Hi, Charlotte,' he says. 'I was in the neighbourhood and I thought I'd stop by and see how you're doing.'

'After all these years you're still calling me Charlotte,' she says. 'Why don't you call me Charlie? You would if I were a walking-around woman.'

'I didn't want to get too familiar,' says Max.

'Nothing stays the same,' says Charlotte. 'You *have* to get more familiar as time goes by.'

'OK, Charlie,' says Max. 'Whatever you say.'

'Good,' says Charlie. 'I agree with what you said to your mind not long ago: sadness is the basic hedgehog condition.'

'I didn't mean to offend you,' says Max.

'You didn't,' says Charlie. 'The thing is, maybe we should put the usual approach on hold for the present and talk about ideas that probably won't go all the way to the bank.'

'I'm with you, Charlie,' says Max.

'Good. Do you remember, we were talking about my

strange dream?'

'I remember,' says Max.

'I said there was moonlight on a river,' says Charlie. 'A full moon reflected in the water, in the glimmers of the water in the night. Strange moonlight, not from now. Moonlight from long ago. The sound of a fish jumping. Close but far away, far away in time.'

'I remember,' says Max.

'Tell me,' says Charlie.

'I was at Scout camp that summer,' says Max. 'My father had died in August the year before. Bugle calls for every part of the day. For raising the flag in the morning and lowering it at Retreat. We slept in tents with wooden floors. I had a little oil lamp I used for reading. Privies in the woods. We had camp-fires where we told stories and sang songs. We applauded the stories by saying, "How! How!" We went swimming in the afternoons. When they blew the whistle and yelled "Buddies!" you and your buddy had to join hands and hold them up together. We did a canoe trip down a river. Was it the Allegheny? I don't remember. There were great blue herons, little green herons, turtles. We slept under the stars. The Big Dipper, the North Star, Orion the hunter. We heard the river in the night, we heard fish jumping. We heard owls and raccoons. In the mornings there was mist coming up from the river. We were in the water a lot. There were councillors in every canoe and we used to have canoe fights. All of us could swim or we wouldn't have been on the canoe trip. We used to turn over each other's canoes.'

'What else?' says Charlie.

'I don't remember any more just now,' says Max.

'Maybe later,' says Charlie.

'Yes,' says Max. 'Maybe later.'

55

THE VESSEL ONLY

June 1998. Lola now has a permit to carry a sarod. She'd been lusting for one of her own, and after the first month of lessons Indira is willing to sell her an instrument. Before owning it Lola had thought of names for it: maybe .357 or Clint or Callisto. Now that she holds it in her hands another name comes to mind: Polaris. The star that is the fixed and unchanging North, unlost.

Indira has said that in addition to the lessons she will need to practise for eight to ten hours every day in order to reach the desired level of musicianship. Lola puts in the hours and makes good progress. Hariprasad has given Noah a nakkara, a clay drum with a skin head; and Noah, with a surprisingly good sense of rhythm, does his best to help his mother.

In the daily lessons Indira listens critically. 'You have advanced faster than any shisyia I've ever had,' she says. 'Already you are using *Kan, Meend, Andolan, Murki*, and *Gamak*. You have musical intelligence, but still the hands are ahead of the heart and the ear is not hearing all that it should. I shall play you a raga of my own composition. It is called "*Smriti*", which means "Memory". This music came to me, I was only the vessel. It came through me but not from me. Do you understand the difference?'

'Yes,' says Lola.

'Listen,' says Indira. She begins to play and sing. The music calls up in Lola the memory of her time with Max. The astonishment of love and the joy of it. The bitterness of his betrayal. The wonder of Noah. The times that have been and the times that might have been. As Lola listens she loses all track of time. She has no awareness of how long the music has been going on. The music is now and the times remembered are now. She weeps, adding her voice to the voices of Indira and the sarod. The music and the singing stop. When Lola is able to speak she says, 'Yes, that's how it is.'

'Whatever you heard,' says Indira, 'was in the music. I did not create the music. I am the vessel only. The music came through me and I did not interfere with it. I think you will understand this with your head but will your heart understand it? Will your hands understand it?'

'Yes,' says Lola. 'I will learn to be the vessel only.'

56

THE ENORMITY

September 1998. Interesting, thinks Lola, how rage and delight can live side by side in her. Rage at Max, delight in their child. Indira's teaching has had something of a civilising effect on her. Now when she thinks of Max she tries to consider his actions more calmly, more objectively than before. But no matter how hard she tries, the enormity of his behaviour still hits her like a two-tonne safe dropped from a tall building. How could he say what he said, do what he did, be as he was with her when he was, as far as she knew, being the same with Lula Mae Flowers? Even the woman's name was a joke. That he should get Lula Mae pregnant while doing the same to her, Lola! How did his mind work, that he could do that? As if she, Lola, were no one special. She who had given him her whole heart, her unconditional love, by the seven stars of Ursa Major and the Hale-Bopp comet. Would the hurt and the anger ever go away or would they grow with time to fill her soul with blackness?

But even while she thinks this her hands, calmer and more peaceful, draw from the sarod the notes of Indira's '*Smriti*'. Lola's voice rises in her to join the sarod. The good moments she remembers, are they truly false or falsely true? Do they flicker like flecks of gold in the bed of time's river? Gold then and gold now? Sifting these grains of the past tires her. The music is coming through her as it had come through Indira. She is the vessel only. The music is more than she is. Noah is crooning softly. The music is coming through him as well.

57

KIRSTY'S FETCH

December 1998. Lola, always interested in place names, has learned by now that the Deil's Hurdies, the cleft formation sticking out of the sea, is (are) the Devil's Buttocks. The Teeny Titties, two small finials of rock near the shore, would be Little Sisters in English. Kirsty's Knowe (Knoll), a grassy hill overlooking the sea, has attracted her because of its story. An old man, a retired fisherman, has told her that the eponymous Kirsty hanged herself when her lover deserted her. He drowned soon after. Since then an apparition called Kirsty's Fetch was said to be seen on Kirsty's Knowe by men fated to drown.

'Has anybody seen it recently?' Lola asked.

'Not that I know of,' said the old fisherman. 'People don't see as much as they used to. I blame the television.'

Kirsty's Knowe has become a favourite walk of Lola's. She looks out to sea and listens to the sighing of the waters. She never sees the ghost of the long-dead girl but she often talks to Kirsty.

58

BOILERMAKERS NO

December 1998. Max and Harold Klein at The Pickled Pelican, drinking Pedigree without Glenfiddich. They want to reach unconsciousness (whether ambulatory or horizontal) more slowly than the last time. 'I hate these cutesy pub names,' says Klein. 'Why couldn't they call it something straight, like The 14 Bus?'

'You ever heard of a pub named after a bus?' says Max.

'No, but I'm sure it deserves to be celebrated as much as the dukes and duchesses you usually see on pub signs.'

'This one used to be The Princess Royal,' says Max.

'There you go. But don't distract me.'

'Sorry. You were saying.'

'I was saying the 14 bus. Let's drink to it.'

'OK. The 14 bus!' says Max.

'The 14 bus!' says Klein. Clink. 'Not that drinking to it helps.'

'I'm not with you,' says Max.

'Of course not. We're all alone. The red keeps changing.'

'The red?' says Max.

'The red of the bus. Something is building up in that old

Routemaster. Some intention rising from the deep like the Kraken. Hop on, hop off indeed. As if!'

'As if what?'

'As if your destiny were something you could hop on to or off.'

'Do you have to take the 14 often?' says Max.

'Not very. Actually the danger is minimal when I'm a passenger. The thing takes on a new complexion when I'm on foot.'

'Redder?' says Max.

'Different,' says Klein. 'You can't tell what they're thinking.'

'Treat the 14 as you would a hostile dog,' says Max. 'Don't show fear. While staying out of its way, of course.'

'Easy for you to talk,' says Klein. 'Why aren't you at home grinding out your next novel?'

'Some grinds are slower than others,' says Max. 'There are times when I find it difficult to concentrate on the writing.' He takes a photograph out of his wallet and shows it to Klein. 'Here's the latest of my son Victor. He was a year old last November 28th.'

'William Blake's birthday,' says Klein.

'Jean-Baptiste Lully's also,' says Max. He and Klein think about this while working on their third pints.

'He certainly doesn't look Jewish,' says Klein.

'His mother's genes seem to have been dominant,' says Max. 'People that see him say "Ah!"'

'Does he talk?' says Klein.

'Not yet. Lula Mae says he appears to be thinking about what to say first,' says Max.

'Cautious,' says Klein. 'Probably just as well. Have you been to Texas for a visit?'

'Not so far.'

'Planning one?'

'I don't know. My fatherhood is a total confusion to me. Sometimes I dream that I have another son.' Max doesn't speak the name of his dream son. Both he and Klein fall silent, lost in thought and Pedigree. Max gets a fourth pint for each of them.

After a while Klein lifts his right hand with the index finger in the admonitory position. 'Remember,' he says, 'Mack in Barch '97, the first time we had drunks here at The 14 Bus, I told you that the best thing . . . What was I saying?'

'The best thing mack in Barch '97.'

'Right. You could do for both of your women was to get out of their lives.'

'I remember.'

'I think the same about your child or childs. Children. As the case may be. If you can't be in the same place with them. Can't be a full-time father. Better off without you. Vanity of vanities. One generation pisseth itself away and another generation likewise. That's all she wrote.' Klein falls asleep. Max wakes him up. They visit the Gents and leave The 14 Bus. Or The Pickled Pelican. Whichever.

59

THE RAINBOW SIGN

March 1999. Max has been doing his best to achieve Page One with whatever he can. Moe Levy has left him and no one has replaced him. Charlotte Prickles is doing what she can to help with river memories but there's been no progress. Max has had times like this before and he's always got through them so maybe he'll get through this one.

This day is not like other days. It's the vernal equinox. It was just two years ago that he and Lola picnicked on Mai Dun. Max is all keyed up, ready for messages from anywhere. Sitting at his desk with a bottle of red, he falls asleep and dreams that he's on a boat. He's on Noah's Ark. He looks at his hands and sees the hands of a boy. Max is the boy Noah, his own dream son. In his hands is the raven. The boy Noah goes to the window. He launches the raven. The raven is Max. He sees the rainbow. He loops the loop, flies to Mai Dun and lands there by the ribbon that Lola tied to a grass stem two years ago.

Max wakes up feeling calm and clear. He doesn't know why or how, but this dream has changed him. He doesn't know if he has a son by Lola. He doesn't know where she is or whom she's with. Doesn't know if he'll ever see her again. But he knows now that there can be no other woman for him.

60

WELL, REALLY, WHAT?

March 1999. On the second anniversary of the Mai Dun vernal equinox Lola does nothing to mark the day. With Noah on her lap she thinks about what has brought her to this day. She had come to Diamond Heart full of rage. Full of hurt. She had taken up the sarod with the aim of composing a raga that would, if she could call up the demon of Forgetfulness, erase her from Max Lesser's memory. But the deeper she gets into Indian music the more difficult it is for her to know exactly how she feels. Certainly the self Max had presented to her had been a lie. But how much of a lie? The first time he saw her he said she was his destiny woman. Outrageous. He said it so loudly that everybody in the shop turned to look at him. Lola was embarrassed. But in her heart she'd been hoping for her fate to declare itself in just such a sudden and startling manner. In that moment she felt as if she'd let go of the trapeze of her ordinary life and was flying through the air to Max's outstretched hands. There was of course a safety net called Basil. But the thrill of letting go and flying like that! What Max had said that day was not a lie, she knew that. And her response was not a lie. Through the air she flew to him, and that was real. That was a true thing.

Where did the lie start? With Lula Mae? Not really. The lie started with Max's constant craving for a bit of strange while he pretended to be true to her, Lola. Could she have changed him? What if he hadn't got Lula Mae pregnant? At some point Lola would have told him, 'It's either her or me. Choose.' That day at Mai Dun, did his announcement of Lula Mae's pregnancy mean that he'd chosen the homecoming queen? She hadn't given him a chance to say what he intended to do. He'd wanted to talk and she'd crashed the E-type instead of listening.

Lola takes up Polaris and Noah, watching her, goes to his nakkara. Indira has given Lola the written-out music for 'Smriti' which is definitely not a piece for beginners. Lola follows the still unfamiliar notation slowly and carefully, but her very hesitancy becomes an embellishment of the shadowy ascents and descents of 'Memory'. She cannot bring to this music any rage or hurt. She can only be the vessel for what her fingers call up from the sarod. Love remembered. Longing and regret. Noah, listening attentively, draws closer to his mother, his drumbeats helping her to find the music.

61

VICTOR'S FIRST WORD

June 1999. 'Dear Max,' writes Lula Mae. 'Victor is a year and a half old now. As you can see from the photo, he's looking handsomer all the time. He said his first word today. "Dada." Daddy. He said it to Jim Bob Baker. Jim Bob has asked me to marry him and I've said yes. I know I promised you that he'd never call anybody Daddy but you, but the reality is that you and he have never seen each other and probably never will. So reality has made me break that promise. I hope you'll forgive me and I think you will. Jim Bob has his own software company and he works mostly from home. He's a good man, he loves Victor and Victor loves him. Don't send any more money. Wish us luck. Love X, Lula Mae.'

62

RIVER IN THE MIND

September 1999. 'Talk to me about the river,' says Charlie
Prickles to Max. 'Tell me whatever comes to mind.'

'Well,' says Max, 'it's pretty much what I've told you. We
paddled. We swam. We had canoe fights. I think we went
through a lock. We cooked over a fire, we slept under the
stars. When we got to the end of the canoe trip a truck took
us back to camp.'

'That's the canoe trip,' says Charlie. 'But what I asked you
about was the river.'

'The river we took the trip on?' says Max. 'I don't
even remember if it was the Allegheny or the Susquehanna
or what.'

'I just mean *river*,' says Charlie. 'The river in your
mind.'

'Oh,' says Max. '*That* river.'

'Yes,' says Charlie. 'That one.'

'It flows to the sea,' says Max. 'They all do.'

'Think about that,' says Charlie.

'I always do,' says Max. 'And then the Ark comes in. It's
in my dreams with the raven and the Noah child but there's
no story in that.'

'You can't get a story out of everything,' says Charlie. 'Some things are just for thinking about.'

63

ANOTHER TIME WITH BASIL

December 1999. By now Lola finds saris more comfortable than jeans for sitting on the floor to play the sarod. She has a quasi-Persian rug (the best she could do locally) and several cushions. Sitting crosslegged on the floor makes for a kind of thinking that's different from standing-up or sitting-on-a-chair thinking. The sky is higher, the sea wider. Time stretches out in all directions.

Noah's sitting near her. He's wearing a woollen waistcoat crocheted by his mother in broad bumblebee bands of yellow and black. Both he and Mum like the effect and sometimes they have little buzzing conversations. Noah's first word was 'deh'. As close as he could get to 'destiny', which Lola has evidently murmured more often than she's been aware of. He's making good progress on the nakkara, and under Hariprasad's tutelage is able to keep the beat with a skill beyond his years. He particularly enjoys the slow tempos and repetitions of the Dhrupad style. He accompanies Lola as she plays and sings, in English, her own compositions. 'Yesterday, yesterday, gone away, here to stay,' she chants. Noah chants along while beating out the time, tunka tu, tunka tu. He likes to play with words. 'Dessa nay, yessa nay, onna way, heena say.' When they come to a pause he says, 'Dad?'

'What about him?' says Lola.

'Where?'

'I don't know,' says Lola. 'London, I suppose.'

'London,' says Noah. 'We going?'

'No,' says Lola.

'Dad coming here?'

'No.'

'Why no?'

'That's just how it is.'

'His name?' says Noah.

'Max,' says Lola.

There's someone at the door. Lola opens it to a rush of cold air and Basil.

'Dad?' says Noah.

'No,' says Lola. 'Basil.'

'Lola!' says Basil. Here he is in his Barbour and cashmere polo-neck, six foot two and ruggedly handsome in a silky way. All the uproar of Christmas in London blows in with him. The lights, the noise, the whole thing. He's turned Diamond Heart upside-down and a little sparkling snowfall seems to come down around him. Mwah, mwah! Big hug. He pauses to clock Noah. 'Yellow and black stripes,' he says. 'But not a WASP.' He reaches out to pat Noah on the head. Noah backs away.

'I told Mummy and Daddy not to tell you I was here,' says Lola.

'You can't blame them,' says Basil. 'They're worried about you, Lo, and so am I.'

'You can call me Lola,' says Lola. 'I'm sorry you travelled all this way for nothing. You must have many things to do back in London. Don't let me keep you.'

'Why are you being so hostile? What's bothering you?'

'*Now* is bothering me, Basil, and I need to be left alone to get on with it.'

'You mean Now with a capital N?'

'That's what I mean: the big Now that includes everything all the way back to before there was anything.'

'Before there was form, before there was emptiness?'

'What do you know about form and emptiness?'

'I had a Buddhist wisdom period when I was about your age, Lola.' He coughs, falls silent for a moment. Then his voice changes. 'Right now what I know is the emptiness of life without you.'

'Don't, Basil. Now is where you mostly don't get what you want. I can say it better with the sarod. Listen.' Lola has begun, sooner than Indira expected, to compose a raga of her own. It has the same title as Indira's: '*Smriti*'. 'Memory'. She begins the first melodic sequence, letting herself be the vessel for what has come to her. Noah is with her on the nakkara. Lola has composed only the opening of the raga but as she plays, she hears more and goes with it. Happiness, sadness, longing and regret. She loses track of time, barely noticing the cold air when the door opens and closes. When she's gone as far as she can with the music she looks up. She and Noah are alone.

64

A FAR, FAR BETTER FANTASY

March 2000. Another vernal equinox. Noticed but uncelebrated by Max. He's working but so far nothing significant has happened. While trying for Page One with Fujitsu/Siemens he takes little mental side trips. He's always had a rich fantasy life but now his waking dreams take on a nobler flavour than before. 'Let's do the train one again,' he says to his mind.

'OK, boss,' says his mind, and sets the scene: some bleak out-of-the-way place under a dark sky. A few ravens croaking around and looking black. A little thunder, maybe some lightning, some Hammer Horror effects. A level crossing with no barrier. Here come Lola and Noah in the E-type. Noah's ten or eleven. Lola looks as she did three years ago. O my God, the car has stalled on the tracks. She can't get it started. Max can feel the vibration in the rails. Now he hears the train. Now he sees it, coming fast, its single white eye boring through the greyness. Doesn't the engine driver see the car? Is he asleep? Doesn't Lola hear the train? She's still trying the starter. Max runs to the car, tries to push it out of the way. The E-type doesn't move. Max puts his back to it, gets a good grip on the rear bumper, heaves back with all his strength. Yes! The car is off the tracks, Lola and Noah are safe but Max falls to the ground and is crushed by the train. His dying words: 'They're safe!'

'Why didn't Lola grab Noah and get out of the car?' says Max's mind.

'Maybe she couldn't unfasten their seat belts,' says Max. 'Maybe she fainted. We can always change the details.'

'Get real,' says his mind.

65

A LITTLE BIT OF NO LUCK

October 2000. Max is of course a little crazier than some. But he's more or less reasonable and he reasons that it's pointless for him to bang his head against a wall of non-communication. He doesn't know where Lola is but she knows where he is and if she wants to see him or talk to him she'll get in touch. In the meantime he gets through the days one at a time.

In his morning reading of *The Times* Max spots an item about a honey buzzard who lost its bearings on a migratory flight from Scotland to Africa. This bird, a juvenile, had only learned to fly a month before. Tracked by satellite, it flew three thousand miles without food or rest. It was thought to have died of exhaustion until signals picked up from the middle of the Atlantic indicated that the bird had landed on a floating object more than two hundred miles from the nearest land. 'Hang in there,' says Max. 'Don't give up.' Next morning there's no news but two days later there's another report. The signals have continued but the bird is presumed dead. 'Dammit,' says Max. Thinking of the honey buzzard's flight he can feel the ardent wingbeats, see the deadly waters far below. 'All those hours with no food, no rest! Lindbergh got a ticker-tape parade and this one winds up dead.'

'It lost its way,' says Max's mind.

'Maybe a little favouring wind was all it needed for a landfall,' says Max. 'Just a little bit of luck.'

66

ARK OF MYSTERY

January 2001. Max still thinks about the honey buzzard, still sees the deadly waters far below. He visits Charlotte Prickles. 'I'm trying to see the river in my mind,' he says. 'It's still the summer river when I was a boy.'

'The river,' says Charlie. 'Sunpoints on the summer water. Dragonflies. The sound of cicadas. You have the bow paddle. Who has the stern?'

'My father?' says Max.

'Your father,' says Charlie. 'Drops of sunlit water dripping from the paddles as you lift them after the downstroke. Your father steering you through the rapids, past the rocks, into quiet water. On and on.'

'To the sea?' says Max.

'Forty days and forty nights,' says Charlie.

'The flood,' says Max. 'Why do I keep seeing the Ark and the raven that flies out from Noah's hands, from my son's hands, from my hands? What does it mean?'

'An understood mystery is no mystery,' says Charlie. 'This is yours. Live with it.'

67

PENELOPE'S WEB

April 2001. The population of Diamond Heart is a constantly changing one. Most who come there stay for two or three weeks and then return to whatever they do ordinarily. Business is good in the autumn when summer slackers resolve to pull themselves together for the coming season. But the rush is in the dark days of winter when nights are long and spirits low. This sometimes continues into the spring.

As various types arrive and depart to be replaced by new ones, Lola has not lacked for suitors. In her years as a long-term attraction at Diamond Heart she's become a challenge to every male who fancies his chances. At the Diamond Heart Ladbroke's the odds have favoured this one and that one but so far no one has reached the winners' circle. Has Lola sworn a vow of chastity? Not at all. Her libido is in good shape but Noah's existence has imposed a critical standard that no one has been able to bend.

They don't stop trying. The latest hopeful is a retro type called Geoffrey who wears a gold chain with an ankh. In London he drives a Mercedes but he makes his annual Diamond Heart pilgrimage in a white Bedford camper decorated with scenes from the Kama Sutra. Geoffrey is a dentist with a moustache and a beautiful jet-black toupee. He has hairy hands. He's always got his Nikon with him and he's been snapping Lola on her way to and from the Ghoshes' studio and on her evening walks. She ignores him as long as she can but one day she confronts him and says, 'I wish you'd stop taking pictures of me. It gives me the creeps.'

'I'm sorry,' says Geoffrey (snap, snap), 'but I can't help it. Your face speaks to me.'

'Read my face's lips,' says Lola. 'They're saying, "Go away."' She's only a few steps from the studio but she'd like to clear away this annoyance and compose herself before going in.

'I'd love to have a proper photo session with you,' he says. 'The shots I've got so far don't really do you justice.'

'I don't need justice,' says Lola, 'only a little mercy. Please take yourself and your camera elsewhere.'

'Do you believe in destiny?' says Geoffrey.

The sarod in its hard case weighs eight and a half kilos, and with a healthy swing and a good follow-through Lola could certainly flatten this turbulent dentist. She changes to a two-handed grip on the case and something like a snarl starts far back in her throat.

One of Geoffrey's hands has jumped on to her arm. 'Think about it,' he says. 'Fate works in mysterious ways. Sometimes both people realise what's happening, sometimes only one.'

Lola shakes off the hand which does not drop to the ground and crawl away but remains attached to Geoffrey's arm. 'I have a large friend who's a black belt,' she says. 'If I phone him he'll be up here like a shot to sort you out.'

Geoffrey's hands fly up in front of him, palms out as he backs away. 'Peace!' he says. 'I can see that you have a lot on your mind. We'll talk about this another time.' He goes off singing, '"I met her in a club down in old Soho, where

186

you drink champagne and it tastes just like Coca-Cola. See-oh-el-aye cola, el-oh-el-aye Lola la-la-la-la Lola.'''

Lola, somewhat ruffled, smooths herself down and goes in for her lesson. Her concentration is perhaps a little more intense than usual. Mr Retro is not the only current aspirant. There are of course others, some of them not at all objectionable to a less critical woman. To these she says, when they suggest this or that, 'I'm sorry, but all I can think about is this raga I'm trying to compose. I really have no time for anything else.'

Lola's 'Smriti' is in a state of becoming; it's becoming her and she's becoming it. The becoming changes every day, and every day Lola discards the work of the previous day. Playing what she's written, she hears a thickness of tone where it should be fine-spun. She hears a tempo false to the impulse of the melody, hears a clumsiness of ascent and descent. She hears the music not voicing what is in it that wants to speak and she shakes her head and starts again. Memory! Sometimes the widening ripples of dark waters, sometimes flecks of gold in the bed of a stream. The blue sky reflected in a lake, the grey sky over the sea. Changing lights and changing shadows always, images dim and deep or sticking up sharp and dangerous. Lola will not stop until this raga lets go of her. And the raga won't let go of her until it has said everything it needs to say.

68

LOLANESSES

July 2001. Max has four Lola songs on CD: the Dietrich one from *The Blue Angel*; Barry Manilow's 'Copacabana'; the Kinks' 'Lola'; and 'Whatever Lola Wants' from *Damn Yankees*. Every now and then he plays one of them, but the song he listens to most is Dietrich's. This takes him back to when Lola came to his place in February 1997 and did her Dietrich routine with the black corset, suspenders, etc. Max is haunted by that memory. Lola was impersonating an actress who impersonated a café entertainer in the Berlin of 1930. *'Ich bin die fesche Lola, der Liebling der Saison! Ich hab' ein Pianola zu Haus in mein Salon!'* Dietrich flings out the song with an adorable throwaway don't-give-a-damn sluttish cheerfulness that is a footnote to Lola Bessington's performance, a flicker of something ordinarily unseen in Lord Bessington's daughter. This image, this flavour, joins the Lola of that winter day in St Martin's Lane and the Dover Bookshop, the coltish Lola with cheeks like cold apples. There are so many Lolas! Flashes of her revolve in Max's head from the glitterball of moments past. So many Lolas, so many moments. Gone.

More and more it comes to Max that he's absorbed very

little of Lola's lolaness. 'What's the first thing you learned,' says his mind, 'when you first started writing?'

'To explore my material,' says Max.

'And did you explore the many and varied lolanesses of Lola? The uplands and lowlands, mountains and plains, forests and savannahs? Did you commit to memory the latitudes and longitudes of the islands and archipelagos of Lola? Her winds and tides and barometric pressures? Her El Niños, for Christ's sake?'

'Some,' says Max, 'but not enough.'

'What,' says his mind, 'you didn't have time? You weren't interested?'

'Of course I was interested,' says Max.

'Interested how? Like when you look at a fast food menu and you say, "Gimme a cheeseburger, large fries, and a Diet Pepsi?" Real deep interest like that?'

'Come on,' says Max. 'Enough already. I'm an idiot and I lost her.'

'No,' says his mind. 'Not enough. You're missing the point. Let's talk about Lula Mae Cheeseburger with the large fries. If you'd given Lola all the attention and interest she deserved you wouldn't have had anything left over for Texas takeaway. Schmuck! That's what love is – when there's nothing left over for another woman. Some explorer you are.'

'You've got some mixed metaphors in there,' says Max.

'I do that when I get excited,' says his mind. 'I can't help it.'

69

'SMRITI'

October 2001. Today Lola and Noah perform her raga for Indira and Hariprasad. Hariprasad has set up his equipment to record the music and will burn it on to a compact disc. 'This raga is dedicated to you, our teachers,' says Lola. 'I have tried to be the vessel only for what has come to me. And whatever has come to me has come through your teaching. Thank you.'

Now when she plays, the sarod and the plectrum come to her hands like old friends. The music is already there, waiting to be heard. Noah has handled his nakkara since infancy. Now, almost four years old, he keeps the beat impeccably, proud to be making music with his mother.

'Smriti' begins so quietly that almost it seems unwilling to leave the silence. The first notes are like leaves falling on autumn waters. Yearning for what has been, tasting the passage of time, calling up faces from the shadows, words from the silence, reaching for departed hands. As it goes on, the raga circles and repeats and lingers over its themes. Happiness, sadness, longing and regret trace their figures with recognition and without anger. This is music that was not in Lola when she first came to Diamond Heart.

When the raga ends, Indira and Hariprasad nod their heads and there are big hugs all round. 'Now,' says Indira, 'you are *sumadhur-ragini*. *Su* means good; *madhur* means sweet; and *ragini* means an expert in rendering ragas. You have given yourself to the music and we have just heard how the music has given itself to you. You are an artist now, and it is good that you are serious about your music. But don't be serious all the time. Have a little fun now and then.'

'Music is all well and good in its place,' says Hariprasad, 'but the main action here is Zen poker. You should come back some time and give it a try.'

'Maybe when Noah's a little older,' says Lola. 'Until then, wherever I go, you'll be with me.'

'And you'll be with us,' says Indira. Hariprasad gives Noah a wooden flute and she gives Lola a copy of *Buddhist Wisdom Books*.

'I'm embarrassed,' says Lola. 'I've had a borrowed copy all these years and I've never read it.'

'No matter,' says Hariprasad. 'Just hold it in your hands from time to time. Maybe not reading it is the same as reading it.'

'My present for you isn't much,' says Lola. 'It's only my notation for the raga I've just played. Maybe it will remind you of our time together.'

'This time with you was itself a gift,' says Indira. 'We thank you.'

Hariprasad gives Lola the CD, good-luck wishes are exchanged, and the years at Diamond Heart are almost at an end.

70

WHAT SEARCHING EYES

November 2001. Lola and Noah take a last walk on Kirsty's Knowe and smell the moonlit sea. Lola's thinking about what she always thinks about when she notices someone else looking down at the sea. A woman, no one she recognises from the back. Dark shawl, long skirt. 'Hi,' says Lola. The woman turns. Only a girl, really, glimmering in the moonlight, almost not there. What a sad face. What searching eyes. Lola says, 'Are you . . . ?'

The other nods or perhaps not.

'Am I going to drown?' says Lola.

Did the other shake her head?

'What are you trying to tell me?' says Lola.

Was that a cloud passing over the moon? Lola imitates what she seems to be seeing and finds herself standing with both hands over her heart. 'Your heart was broken,' she says. 'My heart was broken too. I took up the sarod.'

No answer. Nobody there. Lola standing with both hands over her heart.

'What was that?' says Noah.

'What was what?' says Lola.

'Were you talking to somebody?' says Noah.

'Did you see anybody?' says Lola.

'No,' says Noah.

'Just talking to myself,' says Lola. The E-type is packed. She's given away whatever wouldn't fit in the boot. Polaris in its case is tucked in snugly behind the seats and the Jaguar takes the road for the night journey to London.

71

DESTINY'S DENTIST

November 2001. Lola likes driving at night. She's comfortable with the homeward road coming towards her under the headlights and vanishing beneath her wheels. It's a Monday night, and at 11:40 there's not much traffic into London. After a while she notices headlights in her rearview mirror that keep their distance and never try to pass. 'I know who that is,' she says. The presence of those lights is tiring, and at Heston Services she pulls in for a coffee. The other headlights pull in behind her.

Lola carries the sleeping Noah into the cafeteria with her and gets her coffee. When she sits down at a table she sees Geoffrey, the retro man, waiting for her. 'Don't say anything,' he says. 'I know that you're a deeply troubled person and I know that I've been sent to watch over you. I'll follow you into London just to see you safely home and I'll always be around if you need me. I think I know what Lola wants, and whatever Lola wants, Lola gets.'

Lola shakes her head, says nothing. She drinks her coffee and goes back to the E-type.

72

PHILIP NOLAN LESSER

November 2001. The years since Lola left have been like no other time in Max's life. He keeps trying to understand what's happened, trying to get his head around his life. On the walls of his workroom are pinned up photographs of Lola in London and on Mai Dun, words of hers that he's written down, maps of London and Dorset, thoughts about her that he's scribbled on bits of paper. It's like what detectives do in the movies when they're trying to get a fix on a murderer. After a time Max thinks no, that isn't it. It's what Philip Nolan did in *The Man without a Country*, by Edward Everett Hale. This story was written in 1863 to inspire patriotism in the Union during the Civil War. It was fiction, but so credible that many readers thought it to be fact.

Philip Nolan, a lieutenant in the western division of the army, was a disciple of Aaron Burr, and as such he was court-martialled in 1807 for his adherence to the man who was plotting to overthrow the government. 'When the president of the court asked him at the close, whether he wished to say anything to show that he had always been faithful to the United States, he cried out, in a fit of frenzy. "D---n the United States! I wish I may never hear of the

United States again!"' The government took him at his word. He was sentenced to spend the rest of his life on ships of the Navy where he would never set foot on the country he had disowned and never hear it mentioned. Transferred from one ship to another, he grew old in his exile. In his one chance at restoring his lost honour he took over the captaincy of a gun crew in a frigate battle with the English and so distinguished himself that the Commodore thanked him and gave him his own sword of ceremony to put on.

But the sentence was never rescinded, and Nolan died at sea on board the US Corvelette *Levant*. In his cabin were seen his pitiful efforts to reclaim what he had lost. There was a map he had drawn from memory of the United States as he knew it in 1807. There was a hand-drawn portrait of Washington draped with the stars and stripes. There was an eagle with lightning blazing from his beak and his foot clasping the globe. Nolan left a note that said:

Bury me in the sea, it has been my home and I love it. But will not someone set up a stone for my memory at Fort Adams or at Orleans, that my disgrace may not be more than I ought to bear? Say on it:

'*In memory of*
PHILIP NOLAN,
Lieutenant in the Army of the United States
HE LOVED HIS COUNTRY AS NO OTHER
MAN HAS LOVED HER; BUT NO MAN
DESERVED LESS AT HER HANDS.'

Max searches for and finds the story on the Internet and prints it out. He reads it with tears running down his face. 'That's how it is with me,' he says. 'Lola was my country and I am a man without a country.'

73

HER NAME WAS WHAT?

November 2001. Although Lola has come in very quietly, her mother has heard her and has rushed downstairs to greet her and the sleeping Noah. 'Even asleep he looks so clever!' she says.

'It's a genetic thing,' says Lola. 'But he's not at all pushy.'

'You look different,' says her mother.

'Well,' says Lola, 'I'm four years older than I was four years ago.'

'I don't mean that,' says Lady Bessington. 'There's something else.'

'There's a lot of something else,' says Lola. 'Things change.'

'Of course things change,' says her mother. 'I'm aware of that even with my limited parental intelligence. The thing is to get your changes to connect with the changes around you.'

'I'm working on it,' says Lola. 'I can't really talk about it yet.'

Noah is put to bed. Lady Bessington, seeing that there isn't going to be a heart-to-heart, settles for a meaningful hug and a goodnight kiss. Lola has a shower and falls into a deep sleep but wakes up around six and gets dressed. She takes the CD and her sarod and goes to her car. Why the sarod? She couldn't say, she just feels better when it's with her. She doesn't look to see if the Kama Sutra van is nearby, she refuses to accord the dentist any further recognition.

The streets are dark and quiet as she drives to Fulham. Birds are noisy although the day hasn't properly arrived. She finds a parking space almost in front of Max's house but she hasn't planned what to do next. Knock on the door? No. Just slip the CD through the letterbox? With a note? What should the note say? She'll do a note later. The CD in her hand approaches the letterbox, draws back. Maybe tomorrow.

Tomorrow comes and she does nothing except practise the sarod. 'What if I leave the CD without a note?' she says to herself. 'Will he know it's from me?'

'Who?' says Noah.

'Nobody,' says Lola. 'I was talking to myself.'

Lola's parents are worried about the changes in their daughter. 'Lola dear,' says Lady Bessington, 'I don't want to be intrusive but you seem so troubled. I wish you'd tell me what's weighing you down.'

'It ain't heavy,' says Lola. 'It's my life. Try not to worry.'

Two days after her first trip to Max's house she again leaves Belgravia alone in the early morning without saying anything to anyone. Again she drives to Fulham. With the sarod. 'Why Polaris?' she says to herself. 'Am I going to serenade him?' This time there's a space right in front of Max's house. She parks and gets out of the car with the CD in her hand. She's about to start up the steps to Max's front door when she hears something behind her grunting and breathing hard and there's Apasmara writhing on the pavement like a dog that's been run over. 'You!' she says. 'What are you doing here?'

'You know,' says the dwarf demon.

'Indeed I don't,' says Lola.

'Yes, you do,' says Apasmara. 'You called me.'

'I did not!' says Lola.

'Yes, you did,' says Apasmara.

'Did not!' says Lola.

'Did,' says Apasmara.

'When?' says Lola.

'At Diamond Heart,' says Apasmara. 'You opened yourself to me, you held me in your mind. Ummm. Now you've sent me here to do my thing, yes.'

'Rubbish!' says Lola. 'You may have occurred to me in a moment of confusion but I didn't send you here. Go away.' Suddenly Apasmara does his jumping-spider trick and he's in her arms, cradled like an infant. God! how he stinks. And he's so heavy.

'Hold me,' he murmurs like a lover.

'Don't be ridiculous,' says Lola, but before she can stop him he kisses her and slides his tongue into her mouth. Ugh! She heaves Apasmara off her but he grabs the CD, flattens himself, and dives through the letterbox with the CD in his hand. Lola hears it land on the mat inside.

'Whatever,' she says. She wipes her mouth with no memory of how it got wet, no recall of the whole encounter. She's shaking all over but she manages to drive back to Belgravia safely where she opens the door, steps inside, and faints.

74

WHATEVER

November 2001. 'Have a little chicken soup,' says Lady Bessington to Lola. 'You need to get your strength back.'

'Chicken soup!' says Lola. 'Who are you, some Jewish mother?'

'All mothers are Jewish mothers,' says Lady Bessington. 'Don't be difficult.'

'I'm not difficult, just impossible.' says Lola. 'What's going on here?'

'You're not well,' says Lady Bessington. 'Dr Harley will be here to have a look at you this morning, and we'll soon have you back on your feet.'

'Who are you?' says Lola.

'I'm your mother,' says Lady Bessington.

'Pull the other one,' says Lola, 'It's got ragas on it.'

'Good morning,' says Dr Harley. 'How are we this morning?'

'How many of us are in this we?' says Lola.

'Just you,' says Dr Harley.

'Good,' says Lola. 'I'm not.'

'Not what?' says Dr Harley.

'Me,' says Lola.

'That's perfectly all right,' says Dr Harley. 'I'll just leave you these tablets and I'll stop by again tomorrow.'

Lola takes the tablets, and when Dr Harley has left and her mother is out of the room she tries to stand up. Nothing happens.

The first tablets Dr Harley prescribed were Dozit 20mg. On his next visit he prescribes Wazzit 40mg, Thissnt 20mg, and Ennethin 10mg, twice daily with chicken soup as required.

Noah visits his mum several times a day and plays his nakkara while Lola slowly recovers from whatever brought her down. While this is going on Max visits Istvan Fallok, Grace Kowalski, and so on.

After a couple of weeks Lola gets out of bed one morning while everyone else is asleep. She doesn't know who she is and she doesn't know where she wants to go but she gets dressed and climbs into the E-type and gives it its head. It takes her to Fulham, up the North End Road, through West Kensington, on to the Great West Road, Hogarth Roundabout, and the M4. Motorway miles move towards her, pass under her, the Jaguar purring contentedly and going a little faster all the time. The E-type swallows the miles as the names of towns grow large in front of Lola, small behind her. PUDDLETOWN, says a sign. An arrow points to WEYMOUTH and she makes the turn. Bang! Flap, flap, flap. Flat tyre. Lola pulls over on to the hard shoulder and gets out of the car. It's a foggy day, although she hasn't noticed it until now. She hasn't ever changed a tyre but she's seen it done. She opens the boot and finds the spare but where are the jack and the lug wrench? She was certain they were here but they're not now. She looks in her wallet and her driving licence says Lola Bessington but the name means nothing to her. There's an AA card with a breakdown number but she's got no mobile. She doesn't like to leave the E-type to look for a roadside emergency phone so she can think of nothing better to do than wait by the car. In a matter of minutes something appears out of the fog. It's a white Bedford camper decorated with scenes from the Kama Sutra.

75

THANK YOU, GOD!

November 2001. Still that same morning. 'Hello,' says Max as he picks up the phone. 'Is Lola with you?' says Lady Bessington.

'No,' says Max. 'A couple of weeks ago I looked out of my bedroom window and saw her but by the time I got downstairs she'd gone.'

'I'm worried about her,' says Lady Bessington. 'She hasn't really been herself lately, and this morning she left without a word while Noah and the rest of us were still asleep.'

'Noah!' says Max.

'Your son,' says Lady Bessington.

'My son!' says Max. 'My son Noah! And all these years not a word.'

'I'm sorry about that,' says Lady Bessington, 'but perhaps we could go into it later. Just now I want to find Lola. Have you any idea where she might be?'

'Yes,' says Max, 'I do. Can you pick me up as soon as possible?' He gives her the address.

'I'm on my way,' says Lady Bessington. Lord Bessington is away at a conference, which makes things simpler.

When she pulls up in her Range Rover Max jumps in and directs her up the North End Road, through West Kensington, on to the Great West Road, Hogarth Roundabout, and the M4. The Range Rover swallows the miles as the names of towns grow large in front of them, small behind them. 'How do you know where she'll be?' says Lady Bessington to Max.

'Trust me,' says Max. 'She's all I've thought about for the last four years.' PUDDLETOWN, says a sign, and here are the E-type and a white Bedford camper and Lola struggling with somebody quite a bit larger than Max.

'Thank you, God!' says Max. He launches himself out of the Range Rover and on to the man who's trying to pull Lola into the van. He knocks Geoffrey away from Lola but Max is having a hard time of it until WHAM! Lola swings Polaris with a good follow-through and out go the lights for the dentist.

'Quick!' she says, 'he's got duct tape. Tape his hands before he comes to. I'm Lola Bessington.'

'I know who you are, Lola,' says Max. 'I'm Max.'

'How do you do,' says Lola, standing with both hands on her heart. 'I'm Lola Bessington.'

'I'm Max,' says Max, unconsciously imitating her with his hands on his heart. Having secured Geoffrey, he says, 'Who's this?'

'He's not nice,' says Lola. 'Make him go away.'

Lady Bessington, who is a magistrate, phones the police. The formalities are taken care of and Geoffrey's banged up in the local nick pending charges. While this is going on Max and Lola are standing there with their arms around each other even though Lola in her state of forgetfulness has only just met him. Perhaps some part of her remembers. The fog has cleared and it looks like being a nice day.

So there it is then. Although Max might have done better in the fidelity department, he's had destiny on his side. What happens now? Well, Lola's memory comes back, and she and Max get married at the next vernal equinox: 20 March on Kirsty's Knowe which, as part of Diamond Heart, has approval for such things. The wedding is an odd little affair, done to Lola's requirements. There's no marquee, the whole thing takes place under the sky in which, in this Northern Hemisphere, Ursa Major never sinks below the horizon. It's a civil ceremony performed by the local registrar but Lola's in her wedding dress and looking every inch the bride. Max is in proper Moss Bros regalia. Seamus Flannery is best man. Harold Klein would have been among the fifty or so invited guests but has had a fatal rendezvous with a 14 bus a few years back. Hariprasad and Indira Ghosh are there with several other musicians to play Lola's '*Smriti*'. Noah holds up one corner of his mother's train and a blonde and blue-eyed Belgravia nymphet has the other. One or two of the guests say 'who's that girl in the shawl?' 'What girl is that?' say the ones spoken to. Lord Bessington gives his daughter away with a good grace and Lady Bessington laughs and cries as appropriate. She can't help thinking what a handsome couple Lola and Basil would have made but she has learned to connect with the changes around her. At the end of the ceremony Lola and Max join hands and recite the names of the seven stars of Ursa Major. Lola's looking into Max's eyes as they do this and this time around he feels fully real. They've been lucky too, because it hasn't rained.

The wedding party drive back to Belgravia and this evening there is a proper reception with a big marquee in the garden and a cast of hundreds. Basil was invited but couldn't make it.

The music is provided by The Serenaders, a band who have climbed out of their coffins to schmaltzify the four main Lola songs along with various golden oldies. The young dance to these in the postmodern manner and their seniors do it their way. Lord Bessington regales guests with his account of Max's impeccable behaviour in the rescue of Lola from the dentist. After a certain amount of champagne and private tuition from Max he joins his son-in-law in a chorus of the Kinky Friedman classic 'They Ain't Makin' Jews Like Jesus Any More'. Lady Bessington laughs and cries some more and tells friends and relatives that Max, who is quite well known to an elite readership, is hard at work on his next novel.

As everyday life resumes Lola carries on with her music and she and Noah (sponsored by Daddy) perform at Wigmore Hall. Charlotte Prickles finds her rhythm again with *Charlotte Prickles and the Orphans' Canoe Trip*. And Max is well on his way to Page One of *Moe Levy's Second Chance*. The raven and his father's Noah's Ark join the lares et penates of his new family and are at home there. Apasmara goes back under Shiva's right foot and is looking forward to his next breakout.

In moments of intimacy, sometimes when they're outside looking up at the stars, Lola says to Max, 'I love you but you don't deserve me.'

'I know,' says Max.

A NOTE ON THE AUTHOR

Russell Hoban is the author of many extraordinary novels including *Turtle Diary*, *Riddley Walker*, *Amaryllis Night and Day* and most recently *The Bat Tattoo*. He has also written some classic books for children including *The Mouse and His Child* and the *Frances* books. He lives in London.

A NOTE ON THE TYPE

The text of this book is set in Bembo. The original types for which were cut by Francesco Griffo for the Venetian printer Aldus Manutius, and were first used in 1495 for Cardinal Bembo's *De Aetna*. Claude Garamond (1480–1561) used Bembo as a model, and so it became the frontrunner of standard European type for the following two centuries. Its modern form was designed, following the original, for Monotype in 1929 and is widely in use today.